This book belongs to,

Eileen Gilbert
32
Peggy Barr Ave,
Potty Quinn
Tony Quinn

x.t.c Quinn

Barry Quinn
Aug 6

THE CLUE OF
The Leaning Chimney

Books by

CAROLYN KEENE

Nancy Drew Mystery Stories

The Secret of the Old Clock
The Hidden Staircase
The Bungalow Mystery
The Mystery at Lilac Inn
The Secret at Shadow Ranch
The Secret of Red Gate Farm
The Clue in the Diary
Nancy's Mysterious Letter
The Sign of the Twisted Candles
The Password to Larkspur Lane
The Clue of the Broken Locket
The Message in the Hollow Oak
The Mystery of the Ivory Charm
The Whispering Statue
The Haunted Bridge
The Clue of the Tapping Heels
The Mystery of the Brass Bound Trunk
The Mystery at the Moss-Covered Mansion
The Quest of the Missing Map

The Clue in the Jewel Box
The Secret in the Old Attic
The Clue in the Crumbling Wall
The Mystery of the Tolling Bell
The Clue in the Old Album
The Ghost of Blackwood Hall
The Clue of the Leaning Chimney
The Secret of the Wooden Lady
The Clue of the Black Keys
The Mystery at the Ski Jump
The Clue of the Velvet Mask
The Ringmaster's Secret
The Scarlet Slipper Mystery
The Witch Tree Symbol
The Hidden Window Mystery
The Haunted Showboat
The Secret of the Golden Pavilion
The Clue in the Old Stagecoach
The Mystery of the Fire Dragon
The Clue of the Dancing Puppet

The Moonstone Castle Mystery

Dana Girls Mystery Stories

By the Light of the Study Lamp
The Secret at Lone Tree Cottage
In the Shadow of the Tower
A Three-Cornered Mystery
The Secret at the Hermitage
The Circle of Footprints
The Mystery of the Locked Room
The Clue in the Cobweb
The Secret at the Gatehouse
The Mysterious Fireplace
The Clue of the Rusty Key
The Portrait in the Sand

The Secret in the Old Well
The Clue in the Ivy
The Secret of the Jade Ring
Mystery at the Crossroads
The Ghost in the Gallery
The Clue of the Black Flower
The Winking Ruby Mystery
The Secret of the Swiss Chalet
The Haunted Lagoon
The Mystery of the Bamboo Bird
The Sierra Gold Mystery
The Secret of Lost Lake

Eileen

Eileen

Eileen

Eileen
Gilbert

"We'd better call the police," Nancy suggested.

The Clue of the Leaning Chimney

THE CLUE OF

The Leaning Chimney

BY CAROLYN KEENE

NEW YORK

Grosset & Dunlap

PUBLISHERS

Contents

THE CLUE OF
The Leaning Chimney

CHAPTER I

The Mysterious Stranger

"OH, NANCY, this road is so lonely! And here we are with all this money. It'd be awful if it were stolen!"

Bess Marvin gripped the purse in her lap a bit more tightly and peered nervously through the windshield of the convertible.

A dark forest flowed past the car on either side of the road. Black clouds were gathering in the night sky, and the wind whispered dismally through the swaying trees.

The pretty, somewhat plump girl shivered slightly and sat a little closer to Nancy.

"It's—it's almost spooky," she added in a hushed voice.

"Cheer up, Bess," comforted the slim, golden-haired driver. "We'll soon be home."

Nancy Drew spoke with more confidence than

she felt. As she deftly took the car around a turn in Three Bridges Road, her blue eyes mirrored a slight uneasiness in her own thoughts. She glanced at the purse in Bess's lap. It contained three hundred and forty-two dollars and sixty-three cents, the proceeds of a charity rummage sale the girls had helped run that evening in Masonville.

Nancy, who was treasurer of the group, had the responsibility of depositing the money in a River Heights bank. Studying the dark, deserted road ahead, she wondered if she had not made a mistake in taking the lonely short cut.

The attractive girl tucked a stray wisp of hair into place and put the thought firmly out of her mind.

"Don't be a ninny," she chided herself. "Just because there's no traffic, there's no reason for me to start imagining things."

"Nancy, can't you drive faster?" Bess asked.

Stealing a look at her nervous companion, Nancy smiled with affection. Bess was one of Nancy's closest friends.

There was a sudden flash of lightning, followed by a clap of thunder. A few drops of rain spattered against the windshield.

"Oh, dear," wailed Bess. "More trouble."

Nancy did not comment. The car was approaching a series of sharp, twisting curves in the road just this side of Hunter's Bridge. Driving around them safely required all her attention.

As they rounded the final one, the headlights suddenly focused on a man. He was bending over something in the road, directly in the path of the car!

Bess screamed. Nancy twisted the steering wheel frantically, at the same time jamming her wrist against the horn button and stepping on the brake. There was a screech of tires as the car swerved and came to a stop thirty feet beyond.

"D-did we—?" Bess stuttered, unable to speak the awful thought in her mind that they had hit the man.

Nancy quickly took a flashlight from the front compartment and got out of the car. A man was lying in the middle of the road.

"Oh, Bess!" she cried fearfully. "He's hurt!"

But even as she hurried toward him, the man stumbled to his feet and began looking around him in the road as if he had lost something.

"Are you all right? I didn't hit you?" Nancy asked.

To her astonishment he growled, "Go away!"

The brim of his battered felt hat was pulled low over his forehead and the turned-up collar of his topcoat concealed his mouth and chin. But Nancy could see a pair of piercing, black eyes. Abruptly, he ran across the road and hid behind some bushes.

"Is this what you're looking for?" Nancy called, stooping over and picking up a bundle which had rolled off to the side.

"Put that bundle down and get out of here!" he ordered sharply.

"But I want to help," Nancy protested. "You may be hurt—"

"Listen, sister, I'm okay," his rough voice cut in. "But if you don't get going, *you'll* get hurt!"

As if to emphasize the threat, a rock, hurled out of the darkness, struck the road a scant six inches away and bounded into the ditch.

Bess, who had come up behind Nancy, tugged at her friend's sleeve. "Come on!" she whispered nervously. "He means it!"

But Nancy, her suspicions aroused, turned over the bundle she was holding. As she stared through a large tear in the paper, another rock, well aimed this time, smashed Nancy's flashlight. It also shattered Nancy's chance of getting a better look at the stranger's bundle.

Bess uttered a squeak of fear. "Oh, Nancy, hurry! Put that thing down and come on!"

This time Nancy obeyed the warning and hurried back to the car. Rain was falling in splashing drops as she started the motor. Nancy looked back, but neither the man nor the bundle was in sight.

"Whew!" said Bess as they drove through the downpour toward River Heights. "Next time you stop to talk to a man on a deserted road, count me out!"

Nancy laughed. "He certainly was a queer one," she agreed. "Too bad we couldn't get a good look at him."

"What do you suppose was in that old bundle that made him act so funny?" Bess asked.

"A vase," Nancy told her. "At least, from what I could see, it looked like one. Green porcelain with an enormous red claw."

"Green porcelain with a red claw?" Bess repeated. "That's odd."

"Why?"

"Well, it sounds an awful lot like a vase on display in the window of Dick Milton's pottery shop," Bess went on. "Dick's vase is green, too, and it has a black Chinese dragon with red claws!"

Dick Milton was a cousin of Bess. He had a small shop on Bedford Street where he made and sold pottery. The young man also held classes in ceramics, one of which Bess was attending.

"The vase is beautiful," Bess went on. "Dick didn't make it—somebody lent it to him, I think."

Bess babbled on, explaining about the perfection of the vase with the enthusiasm of one who has just learned how various pottery pieces are made.

"You ought to join our class," she said. "It's lots of fun."

Nancy found her attention wandering. Her thoughts went back to the man in the road. What was he doing in such a deserted place so late at night? Obviously, he had not wanted to be seen. Nancy's car, suddenly rounding a curve, had caught him unawares. And why had he behaved so strangely about the vase? Could it, by some chance, be the one Bess had seen in Dick Milton's shop?

"Why, Nancy, you're not even listening!" Bess's voice broke in accusingly.

"I'm sorry, Bess," she apologized. "I was thinking of that man and how suspiciously he acted."

"I know what that means," Bess declared. "You're itching for a new mystery to solve!"

The rain had ceased and a few stars began to flicker as Nancy drove through River Heights. As she turned into Bedford Street, Bess noted their new direction with surprise.

"This is the way to Dick's shop!"

"I know," said Nancy. "I want to look at his window."

Soon she eased the convertible to a stop under a street lamp in front of the pottery shop. The two girls got out and hurried to the plate-glass window.

Nancy frowned with anxiety as she peered at the clay dishes and bowls displayed on a black velvet background. There was no vase. Nancy tried the door. It was locked.

"The dragon vase has been stolen!" whispered Bess.

"Let's not jump to conclusions," said Nancy as she tried to quell her own fears. "Perhaps Dick put the vase somewhere else for the night. I'll phone him to make sure."

They walked quickly down the street to a corner drugstore. Nancy slipped into a telephone booth and dialed Dick's number. A sleepy hello answered.

"Dick Milton?" asked Nancy. "This is Nancy Drew. I'm sorry to call you so late, but it's urgent."

Dick became excited. "What's the matter?" he asked.

"It's about the dragon vase in your store window," replied Nancy. "It isn't there now. Did you move it?"

"The dragon vase? No!" Dick Milton's voice trembled with emotion. "It was there when I closed the shop. You say it isn't there now? This is terrible!"

"I'll get the police," Nancy offered.

"Tell them," Dick gasped, "the vase doesn't belong to me, and it's worth—thousands of dollars!"

CHAPTER II

A Double Theft

DICK said he would come right down. He arrived as a police car pulled up to the curb and two patrolmen stepped out. Nodding to the girls and the police, the young proprietor unlocked the door of his shop and entered. He switched on the light.

"You say a vase has been stolen?" queried Murphy, one of the officers.

"What kind of vase?" the other put in quickly.

"A Chinese vase," replied Dick dejectedly. "A rare Ming piece over two thousand years old."

"Whew!" exclaimed Murphy. "Let's see where the thief entered. It's evident it wasn't by the front door."

"Then let's look in the back," his companion said.

The two policemen hurried to the rear of the building, followed by Dick, Nancy and Bess.

"Look!" Murphy exclaimed, pointing to an open window in the back of the shop. Marks of a jimmy were visible on the sill.

"Don't touch anything," said the other officer to Dick, who reached up to close the window. "We'll take fingerprints."

Quickly he opened his kit and took samples from the sill and a near-by chair which the thief might have touched as he entered. But not a print was to be found.

"The thief must have worn gloves," Nancy whispered to Dick.

"No doubt he left footprints outside," declared Murphy.

Nancy hurried out the back door with the officers, who threw their torchlight beams on the earth beneath the window. Big, oval prints indicated the thief's feet had been covered with something to keep them from making marks.

"What's your guess, Miss Drew?" Murphy asked.

"Burlap bags."

"And I think you're right."

Suddenly they were startled by a cry from Dick, who had gone back to the shop. They ran inside.

"What's the matter?" Nancy asked.

"The small, green jade elephant!" he exclaimed. "It's gone, too!"

"Oh, dear!" Bess cried out. "Was that loaned to you, too?"

"Yes," moaned Dick. "It was another of Mr. Soong's pieces. How can I ever repay him!"

"Who's Mr. Soong?" asked one of the officers.

"He's a retired Chinese importer who lent me the vase and the elephant," exclaimed Dick. "Business hasn't been too good, so Mr. Soong lent me the pieces to display, hoping they would attract customers to the shop."

"They attracted more than customers," put in Murphy. "And not a clue to the thief."

"Maybe I have a clue," Nancy spoke up.

"And I'll bet it's a good one," said Murphy.

Nancy's ability as an amateur detective was well known in River Heights. People who were in trouble frequently came to her for assistance. At other times she stumbled upon a mystery as she had this one. The first case the young sleuth had solved was "The Secret of the Old Clock." Recently she had unraveled a mystery involving weird doings and spooky séances, in connection with "The Ghost of Blackwood Hall."

"I hope it's a good clue," Nancy replied, and then told the police about the man she had seen at Hunter's Bridge.

"That queer duck must have been the thief," said Murphy. "Come on, Reilly, let's try to track him down. Thanks for the tip, Miss Drew."

After they had gone, Bess asked Dick when he was going to tell Mr. Soong about the loss.

Dick groaned. "This is going to be the hardest task of my life. And after all Mr. Soong has done for me!"

With leaden feet he walked to the telephone and dialed. The shop was strangely quiet as the three waited for the answer on the other end of the line. There was none.

"I guess Mr. Soong is out," said Dick.

"Or perhaps he's asleep and doesn't hear the ring," suggested Nancy as Dick hung up.

"I'll phone him first thing in the morning," the young man decided. "Well, it's late," he said. "You girls had better go home. Thanks a lot."

"If the police don't catch the thief," said Nancy as Dick locked the pottery shop, "I'd like to help you solve the mystery. I'll drop in tomorrow morning."

The next day, when Nancy came down to breakfast, her head was still full of the stolen vase mystery. Hannah Gruen, the Drews' middle-aged housekeeper, noticed it when she entered from the kitchen carrying a tray. On it were a plate of bacon and eggs, buttered toast, a tall glass of orange juice and a glass of milk. Mrs. Gruen put the food in front of Nancy, but the girl sat as if in a trance.

"Wake up, Nancy," the housekeeper said, laughing.

"Oh, Mrs. Gruen," Nancy said with a smile, "I was just thinking about dragons."

"Your breakfast is more important at the moment. Please eat it," Mrs. Gruen coaxed.

Nancy's mother was not living, and the housekeeper had run the Drew household for so long she was regarded as one of the family. Nancy was Mrs. Gruen's pet love. She was proud of the young detective's accomplishments, yet she never failed to worry when Nancy was on a case.

Nancy ate quickly and rose from the table.

"Aren't you going to finish your juice?" asked Mrs. Gruen. "And with the price of oranges what they are today!"

"Squeeze it back into the orange, darling," Nancy teased. "But honestly, you gave me too much. I must go to Dick Milton's right away."

Nancy deposited the rummage sale money at the bank first. When she arrived at the pottery shop, she found the young man in better spirits.

"I told Mr. Soong about the theft first thing this morning," he said. "He was very calm about it all and said the loss was partly covered by insurance. But of course money can't replace such a rare, old piece. And I *must* pay him the part not covered by insurance."

"Any report from the police?" Nancy asked.

"No trace of the thief," Dick answered. "I guess you'd better join in the hunt. But first, will you please do me a favor, Nancy?"

"Surely." She smiled. "Want me to look for another clue?"

"No," he replied. "I want you to take this piece of jewelry back to Mr. Soong."

Nancy inspected the sea-green jade pendant that Dick held in his palm.

"It's lovely," said Nancy. "May I hold it?"

Dick placed it in her hand. "Careful," he warned. "I mended it only yesterday."

"Why, I can't even see where it was broken," commented the girl, scanning the delicate green jewelry.

"It's the last piece of Mr. Soong's in the shop," Dick explained. "There's an old superstition that things happen in threes. I don't want this to be stolen, too!"

Nancy laughed.

"Will you take it to Mr. Soong?" Dick asked.

"Oh, I'd be thrilled. I've heard his home is like a museum," replied Nancy. "I'd love to meet Mr. Soong, too, and have him tell me all about the vase and the elephant. Then, if I ever see them, I'll be able to recognize them."

Dick placed the jade on top of a fluff of cotton in a tiny white box, wrapped it, and gave the package to Nancy. Ten minutes later she arrived at the address Dick had given her. As she parked the car in front of the attractive Colonial house,

Nancy studied it with a pang of disappointment, then smiled to herself.

"What did you expect, you goose? A Chinese pagoda?"

She went up the walk and, lifting the brass knocker, rapped on the door. It was opened by a short, inscrutable-looking Chinese servant wearing a black alpaca jacket. He regarded Nancy silently.

"Is Mr. Soong at home?" she inquired.

He bowed slightly and stepped back to let her pass. Nancy waited in the foyer while he closed the door, then he showed her into a study and motioned for her to be seated.

Nancy sat down on a lovely chaise longue and turned to thank the servant, but he had silently disappeared. Her eyes wandered over the study. It reflected the cosmopolitan tastes of a widely traveled Chinese gentleman.

As her gaze encountered the fireplace, it became fixed on a square piece of tapestry hung over the mantel. Nancy rose and studied the tapestry more closely. It was richly woven, with a Chinese dragon embroidered in black and red against a background of jade green.

"Do you like it?"

A soft voice close behind her made Nancy whirl sharply. Standing in the doorway was a short, gentle-faced Chinese with spectacles and a tiny goatee. He wore a richly brocaded mandarin coat and beautifully embroidered Chinese slippers. His eyes twinkled, and his slippers shuffled softly as he advanced into the study.

"I hope I did not frighten you?"

Nancy smiled. "I'm afraid you did, just for a moment! You're Mr. Soong?"

"Yes."

"I'm Nancy Drew, a friend of Dick Milton's."

"Oh, the illustrious Drew family. I've heard of both you and your father. Please sit down."

After giving him the package, Nancy quickly brought the conversation to the robbery. She told Mr. Soong about the strange man on the road. Mr. Soong looked hopeful when she mentioned the dragon's-foot design on the vase.

"This tapestry you found so fascinating," he said, indicating the cloth over the mantel, "bears the identical design that is glazed on the vase."

He rose and went to the fireplace. "The dragon you see here was an emperor's own emblem. It has five claws. Only the emperor and his sons and Chinese princes of the first and second rank were allowed to have emblems showing dragons with five claws. Lesser princes had to be content with four-clawed dragons."

"How interesting!" Nancy murmured.

Soong fixed his gentle eyes on Nancy. "Did you notice the number of claws on the vase?"

"No, I didn't," Nancy admitted. "But I'm certain it was your vase." She stood up. "I must go now. I'll let you know if I find another clue."

Mr. Soong nodded and smiled. "It was good of you to come," he said in his soft, musical voice. "I have heard much about your detective abilities and I am flattered that one so charming and capable should wish to help me recover the vase." He paused, then went on slowly, "Perhaps you can aid me in still another matter, Miss Drew—you and your father."

"What sort of matter is it, Mr. Soong? I'd like to be of service in any way I can, but if it's a legal problem Dad will know how to solve it better than I."

Mr. Soong hesitated. "To tell you the truth, I am not certain at this moment what kind of problem it is, although it has legal aspects. Suppose I call on Mr. Drew and tell him about it." His eyes twinkled. "With the condition, of course, that he tell the complete story to you?"

Nancy laughed. "That's the kind of condition I like!"

Mr. Soong tinkled a tiny Chinese bell and the servant silently appeared.

"Ching will show you out," the old Chinese gentleman said. "Good-bye."

Nancy returned to Dick's shop and told him of her visit. "Mr. Soong's a fine person," she added.

"He certainly is," replied Dick, stroking his chin thoughtfully. "That's why I want to repay him as soon as possible. It probably will take a long time," he commented forlornly. "The vase and elephant were worth an awful lot of money."

"I'm going to hunt for them," said Nancy with determination.

"But if you don't find them, I'll pay Mr. Soong back somehow," Dick declared. "I must! And I'm sure I could do it if only—"

His fist hit the top of the counter so hard that the little clay dishes jumped.

"If only I could find the leaning chimney!" he cried.

CHAPTER III

A Valuable Clue

"THE leaning chimney?" Nancy asked quizzically. "What's that?"

"I wish I knew." Dick frowned. "It's a clue to some valuable clay. The leaning chimney may be part of a house, part of a factory—or it may exist only in someone's imagination.

"I learned of it by accident. I was sitting in a phone booth one day when I overheard a man talking in the adjoining booth. I didn't pay any attention until I heard 'unusual China clay,' then 'Masonville' and 'leaning chimney.' I tried to hurry my call so I could ask him about the clay, but when I hung up he had disappeared."

Dick sighed. "I've hunted for such a chimney in what little time I could take away from the shop, but all the chimneys I've seen are as straight as a flagpole!"

Nancy laughed, then grew serious once more.

"China clay is the main ingredient for making fine pottery, isn't it, Dick?"

"It's the best there is!" he replied. "Why, if I could locate a valuable deposit of China clay near by, I might buy it cheap, and make the finest of porcelains like the ancient Chinese! Then I could repay Mr. Soong!"

Dick's eyes glowed at the prospect and the worried frown vanished from his face. Seeing the change in him, Nancy determined to do everything in her power to locate the valuable pit.

"Maybe I can help you find the clay, Dick," she said. "I'll try, anyway."

He stared at her in surprise for a moment, then his mouth broke into a wide grin.

"Would you?" he exclaimed. "That's mighty swell of you."

"If what you overheard the man say is true," said Nancy, "the chimney must be somewhere in or around Masonville."

"If it only were!" Dick's eyes looked dreamy. "I'd enlarge my place, install extra kilns and do a thriving business. I can just visualize it all—Dick Milton, Inc., Fine Potteries."

Then he smiled. "Please forgive me for such silly daydreaming. But you see, I would like my wife and baby daughter to be proud of me."

"A little girl? How nice," Nancy said with a smile. "How old is she?"

Nancy noticed Dick stand up more erect. With a fatherly air of authority he said, beaming, "Susan's her name and she's fifteen months, six days and"—he glanced at the clock on the wall—"five hours old. I'd like you to see her, and meet my wife Connie, too, sometime."

"I'd love to," said Nancy, pushing a stray curl from her forehead. "But, right now, before I start for Masonville to look for the leaning chimney and the China clay, I'd like to learn more about how you make pottery."

The tall young man led Nancy into the workroom back of the shop. This was where the thief had jimmied the window.

In the center of the room stood two long benches overflowing with plaster of Paris molds, unfinished clay pieces, a potter's wheel and various jars and cans. Stacked in a corner were huge, round crocks. Dick explained that these contained moist clay which he had prepared for his classes.

"But you can't do so much with it as you can with China clay," he remarked.

"What are those big black boxes?" Nancy asked, pointing to three square, ovenlike vaults on benches to one side of the room.

"Oh, they're my electric kilns which do my baking." Dick smiled. "Come, I'm firing a piece now. I'll let you have a preview."

He led Nancy over to one kiln. Through a

small peephole, she could see a bright red glow. Inside was a small pyramid-shaped object and beyond that was a vase about seven inches high.

"This is the biscuit stage," Dick informed her. "When that little cone which you see in front of the vase starts to bend, I'll know my piece is finished and turn off the heat. After the vase is completely cool, I'll put on a coat of glaze and refire it. Then it will be ready for sale."

As Nancy and Dick returned to the front of the shop, she thanked him, saying she hoped she had not kept him too long from his work.

"Bess wants me to join your class," Nancy remarked. "Maybe I will—after I find the leaning chimney!"

At that moment a customer entered the store, and Nancy said good-bye.

"Keep me posted," Dick called as she went out.

Nancy walked to her car and started off. As it rolled along the road toward Masonville, she tried to figure out what a leaning chimney would have to do with a clay pit. Perhaps the man whom Dick had overheard was talking about two different things. Maybe there was no link at all between them!

"I may be on a wild-goose chase," Nancy thought. "But it's worth trying, anyway."

Almost without realizing it, she found herself on the old road which she and Bess had taken the night before from Masonville. Nearing Hunter's Bridge, she slowed down, then stopped at the side of the road.

"I'll take a look around," she decided. "Maybe I'll find some kind of clue to the thief's identity."

Sliding across the leather seat of the convertible, she stepped onto the soft dirt shoulder of the road. The earth was still slightly damp after the rain. Various sizes of heavy shoe marks here and there indicated to Nancy that the police had made an investigation.

Nancy walked into the underbrush a few feet, searching carefully for anything the officers might have overlooked. As she ducked under a bush, a large drop of water slid from its leafy cup and dripped down her neck. Nancy hunched her shoulders as a chill ran down her back.

Suddenly she heard a faint rustling. Behind the shrubbery a thorny bush with long, prickly branches was quivering violently, as if a moment before someone had brushed against it.

Her breath coming quickly, Nancy glanced at the damp ground behind the bush. Clearly imprinted in the soft earth were a man's footprints!

Was she about to come face to face with the thief who had stolen the vase?

CHAPTER IV

The Secret Panel

NANCY advanced a few steps, then stopped to listen. She might hear the thief, she figured, if he were lurking in the woods. But the only sound in the ominously silent thicket was the sudden, sweet call of a robin.

"I must be careful," Nancy thought. "I'd be foolish to try tracking him alone. But if I don't follow him, I may lose a valuable clue."

As she pondered, her thoughts were jarred by the screech of brakes, accompanied by the sliding of tires on pavement.

Nancy's heart skipped a beat. A sickening thought flashed through her mind. Maybe someone was coming to meet the man in the woods! The two might close in on her!

"I may be trapped!" she reasoned. "What a goose I was to walk right into it!"

23

She hastened toward the road, carefully concealing herself from the newcomer. When she saw the other car she gave a sigh of relief. In it were Bess and another girl, with the boyish name of George Fayne.

"Hi!" George called gaily. "What's the idea of going sleuthing without us?"

George, as well as Bess, had shared many of Nancy's exciting adventures with her. George, athletic and outspoken, was a great contrast to her mild-mannered cousin Bess.

Nancy did not answer her dark-haired friend. She motioned for the two girls to get out of the car quickly and follow her.

"I think I'm on the trail of the person who stole the vase," she explained, starting off.

Bess locked her car and followed the others. Footprints were clearly visible in the woods. But fifty feet farther on they vanished in the thick undergrowth. There was no sign of the man.

"Oh, dear," said Nancy, disappointed.

George grinned. "What did you expect—that he was going to wait for you?"

Reluctantly Nancy turned back. "I know one thing about the man who was here," she said, "whether he's the vase thief or not. He's not very tall."

"How do you know?" Bess asked.

"By the small footprint and the short stride.

Also, he wears height-increasing shoes," Nancy replied, "and they're new."

"Hypers!" said George, using one of her pet expressions. "You slay me!"

"Tell me about the shoes," Bess demanded.

Nancy explained. "These imprints are deeper than the usual footprints, and here's the trademark, anyway." She pointed to the heelprint. "I just happened to read an ad yesterday about these shoes."

"Nancy, what are you up to?" asked George. "Bess told me about the stolen vase and elephant Is that why you came here?"

"Not exactly. I was on my way to Masonville to look for a leaning chimney."

"A what?" George demanded.

Nancy explained about the clue to the China clay pit, and that it might be in Masonville.

"That's where we're going," said Bess. "To that darling dress shop next to the Inn. How about having lunch with us?"

"Love to," Nancy replied. "Meet you at the Inn at one o'clock."

Bess and George hopped into their car and followed Nancy. Entering the outskirts of Masonville, Nancy slowed her car and motioned that she would leave the girls and start her sleuthing.

She drove around the city slowly in ever-narrowing circles, her keen eyes alert for a chimney that leaned, bent, curved or was anything but perpendicular. At the end of half an hour, she was convinced she had never seen so many straight smokestacks in her life.

Then suddenly she saw it. A chimney that clearly leaned at an angle of several degrees!

"This is luck," she told herself elatedly.

The chimney was on a house next to the corner dwelling in a row of old-fashioned red-brick homes. The chimney was the only feature that distinguished the house from the others. The adjoining corner house was boarded up.

Nancy parked the car at the curb in front of the house with the leaning chimney. As she climbed the creaking steps to the porch and rang the bell, she saw a sign in the front window: *Rooms for Rent.*

After a short interval, a white-haired, elderly woman came to the door, wiping her hands on an apron. She adjusted her spectacles and looked at Nancy inquiringly. The girl smiled and said a trifle self-consciously:

"I know this sounds a little silly, but I've been looking for a leaning chimney and the first one I've found is yours. I've been told that the chimney may have some connection with China clay."

The woman looked puzzled. "China clay?" she repeated slowly. "I don't think I know what you mean."

"Perhaps I'd better introduce myself," said Nancy. "My name is Nancy Drew—"

"Nancy Drew!" the woman interposed with surprise. "From River Heights?" When Nancy nodded, she added, "Why, Mrs. Gruen must be your housekeeper!"

It was Nancy's turn to show surprise. "Do you know Mrs. Gruen?"

The white-haired old lady chuckled. "Lan' sakes, yes! I helped Hannah's mother take care of her when she was a little girl." She opened the door wider and stepped aside. "Come in and sit for a while. I'm Mrs. Wendell."

"Oh, I've heard Mrs. Gruen speak of you." Nancy smiled. "I've wanted to meet you."

Nancy went into the neat, old-fashioned living room and sat down. Hastily removing her apron, Mrs. Wendell lowered herself into a rocker.

"How is Hannah? I haven't seen her for some time."

"Oh, she's fine," Nancy answered politely and waited patiently while Mrs. Wendell reminisced about days gone by.

As soon as she could, Nancy steered the conversation back to China clay. Mrs. Wendell sat thoughtfully for a moment, then she said:

"I've been living in this house for several years, Nancy, and never saw nor heard of a pit of China clay anywhere in the neighborhood.

"But—now let me see," she added, moving gently back and forth in the rocker. "I have something that may help you. There's an old trunk in the attic room. It belonged to Mr. Petersen, who sold me the house. He's dead now. The trunk's got some old papers and maps in it, but I've never looked at them."

"Don't you know what they're about?" Nancy asked.

"Well, no. I've been hankering to read them, but somehow never got around to it. Getting old, I guess. No curiosity left."

Nancy laughed.

"Seems to me if the leaning chimney's got anything to do with the China clay you're looking for," continued Mrs. Wendell, "the papers might mention it."

Nancy listened with mounting interest. "I'd like to look at them," she told Mrs. Wendell.

"All right," the old lady agreed. "Just wait till I fetch my keys."

She went to the kitchen, then returned and they started slowly up the long, narrow stairs. Arriving at the third floor, Mrs. Wendell knocked gently on a door.

"I'm sure Mr. Manning, who rents this room, isn't home," she said. "He hardly ever is around during the day."

When there was no answer, she turned a key

in the lock. At that moment the front doorbell
rang.

"Now, wouldn't you know. Every time I come
upstairs the bell rings!" Mrs. Wendell sighed.
"You go along inside. The trunk is in the closet."

Nancy entered the small, one-windowed room.
It was simply furnished with an iron bedstead, a
chest of drawers and two straight-backed chairs. A
washbasin sat on a flimsy wooden stand under a
mirror next to a closet door. She walked across the
room and opened the door.

"Oh!" Nancy gasped.

*A man was just stepping through an opening in
the rear of the closet!*

Quick as a flash he stepped back. A panel slid
across the space and a lock clicked into place.

CHAPTER V

Captured Loot

"MRS. WENDELL! Come here quick!" Nancy cried at the top of her lungs.

Without waiting for the woman's return, Nancy thrust aside a couple of suits that dangled on a rack and tried to open the panel. It would not budge.

Nancy examined the faint cracks in the closet wall that outlined the panel. They might easily go unnoticed in the subdued light. Then she turned to see Mrs. Wendell's startled gaze.

"A man just sneaked through a panel in the back of this closet," said Nancy.

"Well, I never—!" exclaimed Mrs. Wendell in astonishment, then she began to tremble nervously. "I—I didn't even know there was a panel."

Nancy dashed to the window and looked out to see if anyone would leave the adjoining building. Glimpsing no one, she raced downstairs and looked on the street. The intruder did not appear.

"He must be hiding back of the panel," Nancy decided and reported this to Mrs. Wendell. "Shall we break through?"

"If you think we should," the woman said shakily. "There's a hatchet in the kitchen."

Nancy got it and returned to the attic.

"Stand back, Mrs. Wendell," she warned, raising the hatchet.

Nancy gave the secret panel several hard whacks. The partition sagged. Then a final bang sent it flying into the space beyond.

She stepped through the narrow opening. After a second's hesitation, Mrs. Wendell followed. They stood in the attic of the corner house. The room was empty. Whoever had closed the secret panel had disappeared!

Nancy went to the door. It was locked, but the key was on the inside. Apparently the thief had not gone out that way.

She investigated a closet, Mrs. Wendell holding her breath in fear. No one was inside the cobwebby space.

Puzzled as to where the man had gone, Nancy noticed that the room's single, dirty window was half open. Lifting it all the way, she looked out just in time to see a man's hand grip the top of the high back-yard fence, then disappear!

Pursuit, Nancy figured, would be useless. The man had too much of a head start.

"I wonder how he got down?" asked Mrs. Wendell.

Nancy leaned out the window. The answer to the riddle was apparent. A foot away was a rainspout, entwined with heavy vines. It would be a simple matter for someone to cling to the vines and climb down to the ground.

As Nancy turned back into the dim, gloomy room, Mrs. Wendell gave a loud sneeze. The sound echoed through the musty attic.

"Such dust!" she said. "Nancy, what do you make of all this?"

"I don't like it."

Glancing about the room, Nancy's gaze fell on several bundles, wrapped in newspapers and tied with string. They were lying on the floor close to the wall. She bent over one of them and examined it closely. The newspaper was printed in Chinese!

Quickly untying the string, Nancy opened the bundle. It contained a beautiful Chinese vase decorated with lotus blossoms!

She untied a second bundle, then a third. They, too, held exquisite Oriental vases.

Mrs. Wendell stared at the porcelains in amazement. "My lan'!" she burst out. "Where did *they* come from?"

Nancy had a hunch about that. But she decided to say nothing of her suspicions for the present.

"We'd better call the police," she suggested.

"Oh, dear!" said Mrs. Wendell. "I never thought I'd have to get mixed up with the police."

"Don't be worried," Nancy begged. "Everything will come out all right."

Mrs. Wendell went downstairs. She waited a moment for one of her roomers to leave, then called headquarters.

Meanwhile, Nancy unwrapped the remainder of the bundles. Each one contained a beautiful Oriental vase. She had hoped Mr. Soong's Ming piece and the jade elephant would be among them, but she was disappointed.

The Chinese newspapers intrigued her. After carefully unfolding one of them she stuck part of it in her handbag.

Two Masonville policemen arrived, and Mrs. Wendell at once told them of Nancy's prowess as a detective. Nancy smiled and explained what had happened.

"What was the fellow like?" asked one of the officers, named McCann.

Nancy said she regretted not having had a better look at the intruder so she might identify him, but the man had his head down as he was stepping through the opening.

"Looks like you beat us to something big, Miss Drew," said the officer, his glance taking in the rich assortment of potteries.

He picked up the vase patterned with lotus blossoms.

"This one fits the description of a vase stolen from the Masonville Museum last week," he declared. He turned to Mrs. Wendell. "What do you know about all this stuff, ma'am?"

Mrs. Wendell was flustered, but Nancy put her arm reassuringly around the old lady's shoulder and she spoke up falteringly:

"I don't know anything about it, officer."

"Who lives in this room?" he asked, stepping back into the attic room of her dwelling.

Mrs. Wendell told of having rented it to a John Manning six months before. He had asked to be left alone, as he was working very hard "writing a book" and did not want to be disturbed. The secret panel mystified her, she said; she was sure it had not been there before Manning rented the room.

"Manning probably installed it while you and the other tenants were away from the house," the policeman declared. "What does this fellow Manning look like?"

"Why, he's medium tall," the woman reflected, "with black hair and sort of dark skin. He . . .

he spoke very nice, not like a rough thief. Seemed to me like he'd traveled a great deal."

"Umm." The officer pondered, as if mentally reviewing the rogues' gallery.

"Oh, and he has real black eyes," Mrs. Wendell added quickly. "The kind that stare right through you!"

Nancy's gaze wandered around the floor of the room and the closet. Not seeing what she was looking for, she asked:

"Mrs. Wendell, did you ever notice anything unusual about the height of Mr. Manning's shoes?"

The woman looked at her in surprise. "Why, no," she said.

Nancy told the policeman about the unusual footprints she had found at Hunter's Bridge. He agreed that the prints might well have been made by the thief, and that the thief might be the man known as John Manning.

While the three had been talking, the other policeman had been examining the attics in both houses, searching carefully for additional loot. Finding none, he wrapped up several of Manning's personal belongings to study later for fingerprints and compare them with those on the vases. Finally the two officers gathered together the pieces of pottery and started down the stairs.

"Congratulations on a neat piece of work," one

of them said to Nancy. "If you ever want a job on the Masonville force, let us know!"

"I really only stumbled on this," Nancy said modestly. "I came here looking for a leaning chimney and found an attic full of loot."

The policemen looked at each other incredulously. "A leaning chimney?" asked McCann. "And that led you to discover a crook?"

The other officer cocked his head. "I guess that's what they call woman's intuition. I wish I had some of it!"

After the two police officers had descended the stairs, accompanied by Mrs. Wendell, Nancy looked about Manning's room. What a sight! Dresser drawers were pulled out, the mattress overturned, the rug rolled back, the contents of the trunk scattered over the floor. Even the cardboard backing had been removed from the pictures. Manning's suits had been examined also. The pockets had been turned inside out and their linings inspected.

"I wonder if there could be anything the police missed," Nancy mused as she surveyed the room.

True, they had found plenty of loot, but they had not uncovered a single thing that might be a clue to the identity of the thief.

"The floor!" Nancy said half-aloud. The police hadn't examined the floor boards.

Getting to her knees, the girl scrutinized the

rough-hewn planks. Perhaps a loose one might have served as a hiding place for Manning's mail. But every board was secured by big, broad nails used by carpenters sixty years before.

"Nothing there," sighed Nancy, rising to her feet.

Then a thought flashed through her head. "The window shade!"

Nancy had a sudden vision of letters falling from the tightly rolled up shade when she pulled it down. Going to the window, she tugged the cord. The shade came halfway down, but no letters fluttered to her feet.

Nancy made a discovery, however. The sun, streaming through the window, faintly outlined some dark squares on the shade. Excitedly Nancy removed the shade from its little brass fixtures and laid it on the bed.

"This *is* a find!" she mused in puzzled delight.

Taped to the outside of the shade were four pages torn from an art magazine. They were full-color photographs of rare old Chinese vases!

Attached slightly above them were two yellow sheets of paper listing the museums and wealthy homes where the vases could be found!

CHAPTER VI

The Blinding Glare

"THAT's pretty conclusive proof Manning's the thief," Nancy told herself. "I'll take these papers to the police."

It was easy to understand how they had overlooked the papers Manning had concealed so cunningly in the shade.

Excitedly she unrolled the shade another foot. More papers were attached. Each contained Chinese writing done in bold brush strokes with black ink.

"I wonder what they mean," Nancy thought. "They must have something to do with the vases."

Just then she glanced at her watch. Less than half an hour to meet Bess and George! She had not even looked through the contents of the old trunk for a clue to the China clay pit!

Carefully Nancy removed the papers from the shade and put them in her handbag. While she was restoring the shade to the window, Mrs.

38

Wendell returned.   She said the police would send
a man to watch the house, but they doubted that
Manning would return.

"And I got a carpenter comin' right away to
board up that hole into the other house," Mrs.
Wendell reported.

Nancy told of her new find, then proceeded to
look over the contents of the trunk.   Scattered
among some old clothes were a lot of yellowed
letters.   Nancy ran through the correspondence.
Much of it was personal, so she read only enough
to convince herself there was no mention of China
clay.   An old map lay at the bottom, but it was
of no value.

"Mrs. Wendell," she said, "did Mr. Manning
ever say anything about this trunk?"

The woman looked startled.   She pondered a
moment, then replied slowly, "Yes, he talked quite
a bit about it.   He said it wouldn't bother him in
the room and insisted I leave it here.   Why did
you ask?"

"I believe he might have come here on purpose
to look for something in it; something that belonged to Mr. Petersen."

"Oh, gracious!" said Mrs. Wendell.   "This gets
more complicated every minute."

"Don't worry any more about it," Nancy advised, patting the woman's arm.   "Just forget the
whole thing."

Saying good-bye, Nancy went to her car. She drove as rapidly as she dared in order to keep her date with Bess and George at the Masonville Inn. But when she reached it, she was minutes late.

"Well," said a familiar voice behind her when Nancy had parked, "I hope you don't keep Ned Nickerson waiting like this!"

Nancy blushed as George mentioned the youth's name. Ned Nickerson was a student at Emerson College. Nancy enjoyed his company, and had attended many parties with him.

"I just couldn't get here any sooner," Nancy replied. "Wait till you hear about the secret panel!"

Over the lunch table Nancy told her friends what had happened. Bess's eyes grew wide and George said "Gosh!" and "Hypers!" several times.

After Nancy had finished lunch, she showed the girls the photographs of the vases, then copied the Chinese symbols in a notebook.

"We'd better go," said Bess. "I said I'd be home by four."

"Oh, gosh!" George complained. "That dress I bought won't be ready for an hour."

She explained that it was being altered and all the frills were being taken off. George liked her clothes very simple.

"I bought two dresses, Nancy," said Bess. "They're positively yummy."

"Umm." Nancy smiled. Then, with a sigh, pretending to be envious, she said, "I'll be in the shade beside you two at Helen Townsend's party tonight. Tell you what: suppose you go on home, Bess, and I'll wait for George. I want to stop at the police station with these papers."

The arrangement suited Bess, who drove off at once. She took a longer but more traveled road back to River Heights than the one where the suspected thief had been.

An hour later Nancy and George followed but took the short cut. There was practically no traffic. Nancy poised her foot on the brake as the convertible went around the series of twisting curves approaching Hunter's Bridge.

"Do you think the man you saw here was Manning?" George asked. She leaned forward, looking alertly ahead, as if she expected the fellow to jump out at them any moment.

"Either Manning or a pal of his," Nancy answered. "Mr. Soong's vase wasn't in that attic."

"But it probably would have reached there eventually if you hadn't spoiled Manning's plans," said George. "I wonder where Mr. Soong's vase is?"

Nancy was about to reply when suddenly both girls were blinded by a stabbing glare. Nancy threw up her left hand to shield her eyes. Then, as quickly as the glare had come, it disappeared.

"What was that?" George asked.

Nancy stopped and got out.

"I don't know," she said. "But I intend to find out."

"Not without me," George declared.

Together the girls walked to the woods from which the flash had come. It was on the opposite side of the road to the spot where Nancy had found the footprints. Directly ahead it was sparse with saplings through which rays of the sunlight slanted.

A few seconds later Nancy and George came upon a car. It was a maroon coupé with a badly dented right rear fender. The car was empty.

Attached to the outside frame was a rear-vision mirror. It had been tilted, possibly by the jarring trip off the road. On a hunch, Nancy adjusted the mirror. As she did so, she was struck by the same stabbing glare that had blinded her in the convertible. A ray of sunlight had been reflected from it to the road!

"Funny place to leave a car," George commented. "Do you think the owner is having a picnic?"

Nancy circled the coupé, then jotted down the license number in her notebook.

"I might think the owner was having a picnic if I hadn't seen a thief around here," she answered. "This may be a meeting place for Manning and his friends."

As if in answer to her deduction, Nancy and George heard the murmur of men's voices deeper in the woods. The girls started forward.

They stepped cautiously as the voices grew more distinct, taking care not to make a sound. Presently the girls saw two men. Their backs were turned, and they seemed to be bending over something on a log. Unable to hear what they were saying, Nancy and George crept forward.

Nancy's attention was so fixed on the men that she did not notice a dry twig in her path. The next moment, there was a sharp crack as the twig broke.

The girls heard a startled exclamation, followed by a hollow crash, as if something had dropped and broken. Without looking back, the men scooted into the brush and disappeared.

"George, I'll see what they dropped," Nancy whispered excitedly, running quickly toward the log.

"Be right back!" called George, and raced off in the direction of the disappearing men.

Hoping that they would be heading for their car, George plunged into the dense underbrush. She had to get a look at them!

Beside the log Nancy found part of a wrinkled newspaper. On it lay fragments of what had been a small Oriental bowl. Nancy glanced at the newspaper. It was Chinese!

She bent over to pick up the paper and the broken pieces. They might prove to be a valuable clue. But hardly had she put the last fragment in her bag when a bloodcurdling scream rent the woods.

It came from George!

Nancy raced pell-mell toward the sound, which had come from the direction of the car. Her worst fears aroused, she fairly flew, heedless of the brambles that tore at her dress. Finally she came in sight of the coupé standing exactly where she had seen it.

George was not there!

As Nancy stood uncertain under a low-hanging limb, a shadowy figure suddenly leaped at her. The next moment something was wrapped tightly around her head. She felt a sharp, stinging pain and collapsed to the ground!

CHAPTER VII

A Chinese Puzzle

NANCY recovered her senses in a few minutes and got up. Whatever had been thrown over her head had been removed. There was a dull throbbing in her forehead, but her memory cleared at once.

Her first thought was of George. There was no sign of the other girl. The maroon coupé was gone, and for an instant Nancy was fearful her friend might have been taken off in it. But she discarded the horrible thought at once.

"More than likely George was knocked out too," she reasoned.

Picking up her handbag, which lay on the ground, she began calling George's name. To her relief, the shout was answered.

"I'm over here! Blindfolded! My hands are tied!"

Nancy traced the sound. George stood with her back to a tree, rubbing her wrists against the bark to tear off the handkerchief with which they were bound. Nancy quickly freed her and removed the blindfold. George's story differed only slightly from Nancy's.

"It all happened so fast!" George said. She took a deep breath. "I thought I'd lost the men. When I turned around to go back to you, one of them jumped out of the bushes and tied a handkerchief over my eyes. I screamed and tried to tear it off. But another man tied my hands and told me to keep still!"

"Did you see either of them?" Nancy asked.

"Not enough of their faces to identify them."

Nancy led the way out of the woods to the road. The girls, disappointed and chagrined, but thankful nothing really harmful had happened to them, climbed into Nancy's car and headed for home.

Suddenly George shook off the mood and grinned. "Those fellows were pretty dumb," she said. "You have their license number."

"And they left some other evidence." Nancy told of the pieces of the bowl still in her purse. "One or the other of them might have been Manning."

Some time later Nancy stopped in front of George's house, and her friend got out.

"See you tonight at Helen Townsend's birthday party," she said.

"You bet. I wouldn't miss it for anything!"

Nancy drove on to the motor-vehicle office to learn the name of the owner of the maroon coupé, if possible. The man in charge knew her and, after hearing her story, obligingly telephoned state headquarters for the information.

"You just got here in time," he said, while holding the telephone. "We're about to close."

He found that the license plates had been issued to a Paul Scott of Masonville, and that the coupé had been reported stolen that very afternoon!

"I'll bet those men planned to hide the car in the woods until they could paint it another color and put different license plates on it," Nancy suggested to the man. "May I call the police?"

"Sure thing. Use my desk phone."

After Nancy had talked to Captain McGinnis, she drove to Dick Milton's shop and told him about the leaning chimney in Masonville. Dick was disappointed that the clue had not led to a China clay pit. Then Nancy left him and hurried straight to Mr. Drew's office. She had promised to pick up her father at six o'clock.

Fortunately at that moment an automobile pulled away from the curb in front of the building where Carson Drew had his law office. Nancy skillfully guided the convertible into the vacant spot. As she was about to get out, she saw a short Chinese gentleman with spectacles and a tiny goatee emerge from the building.

"Mr. Soong!" she called.

The Chinese stopped and came over to her.

"You're just the person I want to see!" Nancy greeted him. "Can you spare a minute?"

Mr. Soong nodded. He looked very natty in a gray felt hat and a blue pin-striped suit. He carried a handsome Malacca cane. Nancy opened the door and he seated himself beside her.

"May I drive you home?" she asked.

"That would be very kind. I must hurry to keep an engagement."

On the way she told Mr. Soong of her day's adventures. The Oriental gentleman's face reflected his surprise. He could not identify John Manning, but he begged Nancy to be extremely careful in further investigations.

When Nancy pulled up at Mr. Soong's home, she opened her bag and took out the wrinkled newspaper which held the broken fragments of a Chinese bowl. But first she showed him the symbols she had copied. Mr. Soong looked in amazement at the strange assortment.

"I hope they're not as mystifying to you as they are to me," Nancy remarked.

"It is no mystery what they mean," he replied.

He translated one of the symbols on the sheet, pointing his finger at each character in turn as he spoke.

"Made in the studio of deep peace."

Nancy looked at him, perplexed, but he went on to another group of characters. Again he traced the Chinese characters as he translated.

"Made for the hall of fragrant virtue."

Mr. Soong smiled at Nancy's puzzled expression.

"Each set of symbols is a sort of Chinese hallmark," he explained. "That is to say, they're like the little mark an American manufacturer sometimes stamps on his products to show they are genuine and of good quality."

"I know what you mean," Nancy interposed. "I've seen such marks stamped on silver and gold to testify to their purity."

Mr. Soong nodded in quick agreement, then continued:

"Such symbols have been used for centuries by the Chinese to designate an article as authentic and of fine workmanship," he said. "They go back centuries to the great Sung, Ming and Ch'ing dynasties."

"How interesting!" said Nancy.

The old gentleman peered again at the symbols.

"These particular sets of markings are very old and famous," he informed the girl. "They are from the Ming dynasty and are well known to all experts on porcelains."

"Oh!" exclaimed Nancy. "I'm learning more than I had hoped!" Her brows knit in a frown. "But what use would Manning have for copies of the markings?" she persisted. "And why should he take such pains to conceal them?"

Mr. Soong gave a gentle shrug and smiled. "That I do not know."

Nancy showed him the Chinese newspaper she had taken from the attic in Masonville. It was a Chinese daily published in New York, Mr. Soong told her.

"This Mr. Manning may work with Chinese in New York," he suggested.

Next, Nancy opened the wrinkled newspaper which held the fragments of the broken bowl. The paper, Nancy saw, was the same as the other.

Mr. Soong examined the pieces with great interest, but they were so small he could tell only that the bowl had been made of excellent clay.

The old gentleman looked at Nancy inquiringly, as if to ask for more information. But she shook her head with a sigh.

"They're all the leads I have—this time!" she replied.

Mr. Soong stepped from the car and gravely shook Nancy's hand.

"You have done very well, Miss Drew," he said softly. With both members of your illustrious family trying their best to help me, I am confident that my unworthy problems will soon be solved."

As the Chinese made her a little bow and entered his home, Nancy looked after him, puzzled.

"Now, what did he mean by that?" she asked herself.

The girl hurried back to her father's office building. While she was trying to squeeze into a parking space, a familiar voice said:

"Mind if I take you home?"

Nancy looked around swiftly.

"Dad!" she cried.

She planted a kiss on his cheek, as he got in. Carson Drew was a tall, handsome man of middle age, with alert blue eyes like those of his daughter. Like Nancy's, too, they twinkled when his sense of humor was aroused.

The relationship between Nancy and her father was warm and companionable. He had been a widower since Nancy was ten. She was his only child. Mr. Drew, though a brilliant criminal lawyer, always had time to discuss Nancy's cases with her.

Now, driving home, the distinguished-looking attorney and his attractive daughter talked about her latest adventures. But as Nancy swung the convertible into the driveway of the Drew home, she remembered Mr. Soong's parting words. Nancy repeated them to her father and asked if he knew what they meant.

"You bet I do," he told her. "Mr. Soong paid me a visit today. He wants you and me to undertake a search."

"A search?"

"That's right.   A Chinese puzzle that goes back five years!"

He got out of the car and Nancy quickly followed him.

"Dad, stop keeping me in suspense!" she begged. "What's it all about?"

"I'll tell you the details at dinner," he promised, mounting the steps to the porch.   "It's the story of the missing Engs!"

CHAPTER VIII

The Vanishing Vase

"WHAT are the missing Engs?" Nancy demanded, when she and her father were seated at dinner. "Some valuable jewels?"

Mr. Drew laughed. "You're not even warm!" he teased. "The Engs are Chinese friends of Mr. Soong; Eng Moy and his daughter, Eng Lei. As you know," he added, "Chinese last names come first!"

Carson Drew paused for a moment.

"Go on, Dad," Nancy begged impatiently. "What about the Engs?"

"Five years ago, Eng Moy wrote to Mr. Soong from China. He said he and his daughter were leaving on a trip to the United States and hoped to visit him. According to Mr. Soong, Eng Moy was a well-known maker of porcelains in China. The purpose of his trip was to study American pottery methods."

"Did Eng Lei make pottery, too?" Nancy asked.

Her father shook his head. "Not at the time the Engs left China, at any rate. She was only twelve years old when they sailed. That means she's about seventeen now."

"When did they disappear?" Nancy queried, interested at once in hearing about a girl so close to her own age.

"That's coming. Eng Moy continued to write to Mr. Soong," the lawyer explained. "Eng described tours they had taken through pottery plants in several American cities. Each succeeding letter was postmarked a little closer to River Heights. Finally, Mr. Soong received a letter saying they would visit him the following week."

The lawyer paused.

"And they didn't come?" Nancy asked.

"No. That was four and a half years ago. Mr. Soong hasn't heard from the Engs since!"

"It wasn't very polite," Nancy remarked. "But maybe something happened so they couldn't write."

"That's what Mr. Soong would like to find out," Mr. Drew told his daughter. "He came to my office today because he had received a letter from a relative in China. Mr. Soong supposed the Engs had returned to the Orient without paying him the promised visit. He had been a bit perplexed when his letters to China were never acknowledged."

"Sounds very strange," said Nancy.

"He learned something from the letter he received today," continued the lawyer. "The relative wrote that the Engs never had returned to China and the United States authorities could not account for it."

"Then the Engs are probably still in this country," Nancy reasoned.

"Seems that way," her father agreed. "Mr. Soong fears his friends have met with, well, let's call it foul play. But I'm not so sure."

"What do *you* suspect happened to them?" Nancy asked.

"I don't suspect anything, yet," Mr. Drew replied. "But there are several reasons why some aliens want United States authorities to lose track of them. Espionage is one. Receiving and selling smuggled goods is another. It's even possible that Eng committed a crime in China and fled to America before it was detected."

"Not a friend of Mr. Soong!" said Nancy, shocked.

Her father smiled dryly. "You're probably right, but that doesn't solve the mystery."

Nancy looked at her father searchingly, then asked how she might help on the case.

Mr. Drew smiled affectionately. "As soon as I get a clue, I'll put you to work on it."

"Thanks, Dad." Nancy looked at her watch

and gave a start. "My goodness, I've got to run or I'll be late for Helen's birthday party!"

She popped a peppermint into her mouth and dashed upstairs to dress. Twenty-five minutes later Nancy hurried down, blew a kiss to her father and waved good-bye to Mrs. Gruen.

"Wait a moment," the housekeeper said as she hurried up to Nancy. The girl looked puzzled. Mrs. Gruen continued, her hand holding Nancy's, "I think you're going out alone too many nights, Nancy. And why, pray tell, didn't the Townsends have their birthday party this afternoon?"

Nancy tweaked the end of Mrs. Gruen's nose affectionately. "Because," she replied, "Mr. Townsend wanted to be in on the party."

"I don't blame him," put in Mr. Drew. "He probably wants to be sure of a piece of birthday cake."

Mrs. Gruen was not satisfied. "You worry me, Nancy," she said. "You may be late and I don't like your coming home alone."

"I'll soon settle this," Mr. Drew declared. "Hannah, I'll drive my daughter and her friends to the party and go back for them later."

He and Nancy went out the kitchen door to the garage. Twenty minutes later he dropped Bess, George and Nancy across town, saying he would come back for them later. The other guests welcomed the girls with a chorus of "Where've you been?" and "We'd begun to think you weren't coming!"

Helen Townsend smiled as she approached them and said, "If I know Nancy, she probably was tracking down something."

"That's right." Nancy laughed. "A new way to say 'Happy Birthday.' "

She went upstairs with Bess and George to take off her coat. In five minutes they joined the others in the living room where there was such a buzz of conversation Helen could hardly start the games she had planned. Several were hilarious, and Nancy enjoyed herself immensely.

Finally, during a lull, Bess, looking very cute in a pale-pink taffeta she had bought that afternoon in Masonville, whispered to Nancy, "Did you see it?"

"See what?" asked Nancy, excited. Perhaps Bess had stumbled on some new information to do with the mystery.

Bess leaned closer. "Did you see that luscious layer cake on the dining-room table?"

"Oh, Bess!" said Nancy with a laugh.

As if they had overheard Bess, Helen and Mrs. Townsend ushered the girls into the dining room where cake and ice cream awaited them. About to follow, Nancy noticed an exquisite vase on a shelf of the bookcase. She lifted it carefully and examined the porcelain.

It was in a lovely shade of brown, showing a peach tree at the edge of a sparkling blue lake. An ancient Chinese, attired in a richly brocaded robe, sat under the tree beside a deer.

Nancy studied the bottom of the base. Painted with small, black brush strokes were several Chinese symbols. They seemed to be the same as one set of characters she had copied from the sheets in Manning's room!

Nancy raced upstairs and got her purse. Then, sitting down at a desk, she carefully copied the symbols, blotted the paper and slipped it into her purse.

She was about to replace the old vase in the bookcase when her eye was caught by two strange marks cunningly worked into the leaves of the peach tree. Nancy stared at the small, barely visible markings. The more she looked the more puzzled she became. Before she could copy the little symbols, Mrs. Townsend hurried into the living room.

"Nancy, come on!" she coaxed. "Your ice cream is melting!"

Nancy took the vase and set it back on the shelf.

"Like it?" asked Helen's mother.

"Love it!" Nancy replied. "It's one of the loveliest vases I've ever seen."

"It's a Ming vase. Harry gave it to me for an anniversary present," Mrs. Townsend said, glancing fondly at her husband, who was in the dining room concentrating on his piece of birthday cake.

Nancy sat down to her ice cream and cake, all the while thinking of what she had just discovered. Bess, well into her second helping, was the target of good-natured teasing from the other girls, who were "concerned" about her weight.

Finally, in response to a growing clamor, Helen unwrapped her gifts. "Ohs" and "Ahs" greeted each gaily wrapped package. Helen was as excited as a little girl under a Christmas tree. Besides several pieces of beautiful lingerie, she received an attractive figurine Bess had made in Dick Milton's pottery class.

"Oh, it's lovely," she said. "Thanks heaps Bess."

There was a roar of laughter as a baseball glove from George was opened. But this was something Helen had said she wanted, months before, and no one would give it to her!

Nancy's gift was the surprise of the evening. She had prearranged with Mrs. Townsend that it would be brought in last. Cuddled on a cushion in a little pink basket was a fluffy white kitten.

"Nancy, you darling!" Helen burst out. "You remembered I've been meaning to get one."

The girls gathered around to admire the pet. Then, as the hands of the clock moved toward eleven-thirty, the guests said they must leave.

In twos and threes, the girls trooped upstairs for their coats and purses. When Nancy came down, she went to the desk to get her handbag which she had laid there, and stopped short in surprise. The bag was gone!

She searched the top of the desk thoroughly, and when Mrs. Townsend and the others came downstairs Nancy asked them if they had seen the purse. But none of them knew anything about it.

"What could have become of it?" Mr. Townsend asked, joining the search.

He decided Nancy probably had dropped it in the dining room, and went to look under the table. The purse was not on the floor.

"Find it?" he asked, coming back to the living room.

"No," his wife replied. "I can't imagine what's become of it."

At this moment Nancy noticed that the window near the desk was partly open. Could someone have reached in and taken the bag?

"May I have a flashlight?" she asked.

Obtaining a flashlight from Mr. Townsend, she dashed out the front door and went around to the side of the house, followed by the others. Under the partly opened window was a flower bed. In it were footprints!

At that moment she heard Mrs. Townsend call, "Isn't this your purse, Nancy?"

Nancy turned. Helen's mother was holding out a familiar blue handbag.

"Yes, that's mine," Nancy said. "Thank you. Where did you find it?"

"It was lying here in the grass," Mrs. Townsend explained.

"Oh, I hope nothing's gone," said Helen.

Nancy opened the bag, feeling sure all the contents would be missing. At first glance it seemed as if only the money in it were gone. Then she realized that the paper on which she had copied the Chinese symbols from the vase was also missing.

Suddenly Nancy was struck by a dismaying thought. Without a word, she darted into the house. Her worst fears were confirmed.

The Townsends' beautiful, rare vase had vanished!

CHAPTER IX

Three on a Clue

NANCY stared in dismay at the vacant spot on the shelf. Then she ran into the kitchen, snapped on the back-yard light, and dashed outside. Nobody was there.

By then Mr. and Mrs. Townsend and the girls had caught up to her. "What's the matter now, Nancy?" asked Mr. Townsend.

As she told them about the stolen vase, Nancy felt a sudden twinge of guilt. If the thief had not observed her copying the Chinese symbols on the bottom of the vase, he might never have stolen it. But why was her copy of the symbols so important to him?

Suddenly Nancy thought she knew. Racing back to the side of the house, she fully expected to see the same identifying footprints she had spotted at Hunter's Bridge; prints she believed

62

were Manning's. But she was disappointed. These marks were short and wide.

When she told Bess and George the idea she had had about the footprints, George was inclined to think the thief was some pal of Manning's, nevertheless.

"He's probably one of those men in the woods," she added.

"And has been told to trail you, Nancy," Bess said fearfully. "You'd better give up this mystery."

The Townsends and the others insisted upon hearing about the case. Nancy told what she deemed necessary, and Mr. Townsend went to telephone the police.

"Hypers!" said George. "This puts a damper on everything. And just when we'd had such a wonderful time."

The other girls murmured in agreement. Thanking Helen and her mother for the party, most of them quietly left the house.

Suddenly a thought flashed through Nancy's mind. She went to the desk and picked up the small blotter she had used to dry the ink on her notation of the Chinese characters. They were clearly reproduced in reverse.

"I'll take the blotter home and compare the symbols with those on the other paper," she decided.

Nancy slipped the blotter into her purse and turned back to find Mr. Townsend waiting for her at the door. He told her the police had promised to do everything they could to catch the thief.

"Where did you buy the vase, Mr. Townsend?" Nancy inquired.

"Why, let me see," he replied, reaching into his inside coat pocket. "I think I have the name of the shop right here in my wallet."

He took out a morocco-leather billfold from which he drew a small card.

"Yes, here it is. Sen-yung's Oriental Gift Shop, Madison Avenue, New York." Nancy made a mental note of the name.

Mr. Drew arrived to take the girls home. Upon hearing the story of the theft, and the possibility that Nancy had been spied upon, he was doubly glad he had escorted her to the party and back.

When they reached home, the two sat down in the library for a few minutes to discuss the strange turn of events. Nancy took the blotter from her purse and handed it to her father. Then she went to her room to get a hand mirror and the sheet of paper containing the Chinese symbols found in Manning's room. Holding the blotter up to the mirror, she saw at a glance that the writing was the same as one set of characters on the sheet. It read:

"Made for the hall of fragrant virtue."

Nancy was thrilled at the new clue. But she was

still puzzled over the thief's motive for stealing her copy of the symbols.

"Let the police find that out," Mr. Drew advised her. "You stick to a mystery less dangerous."

In the morning Nancy telephoned to the Townsends, not only to say again how lovely the party had been, but to ask if there was any news of the thief.

"Not a speck," Helen replied. "Say, Nancy, maybe you could find the thief for us."

"If I get any clues, I'll let you know," Nancy promised, and hung up.

Since she could think of no way at the moment to trace the thief, Nancy decided to concentrate on finding the China clay pit. She turned her steps toward the River Heights Library to scan books on local geology. But after poring over many volumes and maps, Nancy had learned nothing.

She closed the books with a sigh and put them back on the shelf. Miss Carter, the librarian, had noticed Nancy's futile search.

"Couldn't you find what you're looking for?" she inquired pleasantly.

Nancy shook her head and told the librarian the nature of her quest.

"Why don't you ask Miles Monroe?" Miss Carter suggested. "He's a retired professor of geology. If anyone knows of a clay deposit, he should. I'll give you his address."

"Thank you," Nancy said, smiling. "I'll go to see him at once."

The geologist lived in a small apartment house two blocks from George Fayne's home. Nancy took the self-service elevator to the top floor. The professor's apartment was just opposite the elevator. She pushed the buzzer under Miles Monroe's name card and in a moment a small peephole flew open. An eye stared at Nancy.

"If you're selling something," boomed a voice, "I don't want any of it!"

Nancy stifled a laugh.

"I'm not a saleswoman," she said. "I came to see you about a geology problem!"

The eye stared a moment longer. Then the peephole snapped shut and the door flew open. A man stood in the doorway, looking Nancy up and down. He was tall and slightly stoop-shouldered, with a sharp, inquisitive face and a thatch of bristling red hair.

"Geology problem!" he snorted. "You're much too pretty for such heavy thoughts. Ought to be home planning for the time when you'll get married. But come in!"

Nancy, amused, followed the professor's long, limping strides into the living room.

"Have a chair!" he said. Mr. Monroe seated himself, looking straight at Nancy. "Well, young lady," he asked, "what's on your mind?"

After Nancy introduced herself, she told of her search for a deposit of China clay. Monroe said he knew of none in the state.

"I've been told," Nancy went on, "that it may be identified in some way with a leaning chimney."

"What nonsense!" Miles Monroe scoffed. "First time I ever heard of using a chimney to find a vein of kaolin! Must be a new technique."

"Kaolin?" repeated Nancy.

The professor replied, "That's what geologists call the fine white clay used in the manufacture of china and porcelain. The name comes from the Chinese *Kaoling*. It's a mountain in China which yielded the first kaolin."

Nancy eagerly absorbed this new knowledge as Miles Monroe added:

"Kaolin is formed by the weathering of granite and other rocks. Then the clay is washed free of the quartz and mixed with feldspar, flint and so forth to make porcelain." He smiled wryly. "You may as well know what it's all about if you're looking for the stuff."

"Of course," Nancy agreed. "But I had hoped you'd be able to tell me about a pit of China clay in this region. It's supposed to be near Masonville."

Professor Monroe rubbed his long nose. "Don't know much about the land around Masonville," he replied. "Had to give up my field trips when I injured my leg in a fall six years ago. That's when I retired. Before that I lived in Philadelphia."

"Well, I'm sorry to have bothered you," Nancy said, rising.

"Say, wait a minute," Miles Monroe burst out suddenly. "There's one section I had an interest in and was always going to get to. It's a stretch of woods several miles out of River Heights toward Masonville."

He gave her directions for reaching it.

"There's an abandoned Civil War iron mine and smelter out there, I was told. It may have a leaning chimney. If you find a China clay pit, I would like to know about it."

Nancy thanked him for the information. She was glad to have the lead, slim as it was.

Professor Monroe limped to the door with her, and she went down to her car. In a few minutes she drove up in front of George's home.

Her friend was mowing the front lawn. Seated on the ground was Bess, languidly clipping a hedge. Both cousins wore blue jeans and rough work shirts, topped off by colored scarves wrapped around their heads.

Nancy tooted her horn. The two girls looked up and ran to the car.

"I'm going for a short drive in the country. Just got a new lead on the leaning chimney," Nancy told them. "Want to come along?"

Bess eyed her friend suspiciously. "What do we have to do?" she asked.

"What difference does it make as long as it's fun!" scoffed George. She slid into the seat beside Nancy.

Bess hesitated. "But I can't go looking like this!" she protested.

"We're not going to a party." Nancy laughed. "Just the woods."

"Okay. I'll go tell your mother, George, where we're going."

She took a moment to grab up coats on her way, then hopped into the convertible. Nancy wheeled away from the curb and headed straight for Three Bridges Road.

"Oh, my goodness!" Bess exclaimed as they neared Hunter's Bridge. "This awful place again!"

"But this time we're not stopping," Nancy reassured her, and Bess sighed in relief.

Shortly after crossing Hunter's Bridge they came to a narrow gravel road which veered to the right. Nancy turned the car onto it.

After traveling about eight miles from River Heights, she pulled up under a tree and stopped. The three girls got out and started through the woods in their search for the abandoned Civil War mine.

They walked for nearly an hour among trees

and through stony pastures, climbing old, rotted fences and slapping at insects. Bess's enthusiasm began to deflate.

"I'm tired," she moaned. "Let's go back. I'll bet Professor Monroe doesn't know what he's talking about."

Even George and Nancy wondered whether the old mine really existed.

"Just a little farther," Nancy urged.

"We'll be in the next state," joked George. "But I'm willing."

The three trudged on, when suddenly a barrier loomed up ahead. It was a high, board fence, topped by strands of rusty barbed wire. The three girls stopped and stared in amazement.

"Why would anyone put up such a thing in this wilderness?" Bess asked.

The girls inspected the fence closely. It was about ten feet high. The boards adjoined one another so snugly that only the narrowest of cracks appeared between them. Nancy tried to peer through one to see what lay on the other side, but she could make out nothing.

"Hypers!" exclaimed George. "The fence must be five hundred feet long!"

"Come on," Nancy urged. "Let's try to find an opening we can see through."

The girls walked along the fence, their eyes probing for a gate or a wide crack.

"Here's the end of the fence," announced Nancy, who was in the lead.

Indeed, it looked like the end, but it was only the end of one side. The board barrier turned sharply at a right angle and continued another two hundred and fifty feet.

"My goodness," Bess complained. "These boards are getting monotonous."

"Don't get bored, darling," punned George. "You've a job to do."

She and Nancy walked on, still looking for an opening. There was not a crack, a peephole or a door.

Bess followed reluctantly. "My poor, aching feet!" she sighed.

"Oh, be quiet!" George chided her. "You ought to be glad they're getting some exercise!"

"If it wasn't for my cousin Dick, I wouldn't go a step farther," Bess declared.

When the girls arrived at the middle of the second stretch of fence, Nancy's eyes fell on a small knothole.

"At last!" she exclaimed.

Stepping up eagerly, she closed one eye and peeked through the hole with the other. At first she was unable to see much because of a growth of trees and bushes. Then, shifting her gaze, Nancy noticed an old, battered brick wall running parallel to the fence, a short distance back from it. The wall was about eight feet high and was topped by a sloping roof. Obviously it was part of a building. But within the range of her vision Nancy could see no windows.

"Find anything?" George asked impatiently.

"Only an old—" Nancy stopped speaking as her eye caught sight of something jutting from the roof of the building. Then she cried excitedly:

"Girls, it's a leaning chimney!"

CHAPTER X

Mystery in Manhattan

"LET me see!" George exclaimed excitedly.

Nancy stepped aside so the dark-haired girl could look through the knothole.

"Maybe it's the abandoned iron mine and smelter!" put in Bess.

"Can't tell from here," George said. "There are so many trees, it's hard to see just what's inside."

"If this is *the* leaning chimney we're looking for," Nancy reasoned, "the China clay pit must be somewhere near by; possibly inside the fence."

"Then all we have to do," George declared, "is get in."

"Let's go," suggested Nancy, starting along the enclosure. "There *must* be an opening somewhere."

"You lose," retorted George as the trio rounded the edge of the fence.

No opening was in sight. Instead, the unbroken

expanse of boards extended another five hundred feet.

When the girls reached the end of this, the fence took another right angle turn. This time it stretched two hundred and fifty feet.

Bess groaned. "Oh, I'm so tired—and hungry."

"Perhaps," teased George, "there's a baseball park inside. If there is, we'll stop at the frankfurter stand."

"Looks to me as if we'll need a helicopter to get inside," Nancy joked, examining the boards closely. "These planks are certainly fitted tight together."

As they walked on, she kept turning over in her mind several things that mystified her: the air of secrecy about the enclosure, the seeming lack of doors and the apparent lack of activity.

The trio finally found themselves back at the point where they had glimpsed the leaning chimney.

"Since we can't get in," Nancy said, "I'm going to try looking inside to see if I can spot any clay pit."

Making her way to a near-by tree, she shinned up to the first branch, then swung herself into the crotch of the tree.

"Find anything?" George asked.

"I can't see much better from here," Nancy reported. "Too many trees inside."

Suddenly she was struck by something near the top of the leaning chimney. It was a rusted iron ornament fastened to the bricks.

"What does it look like?" asked George when Nancy reported her discovery.

"A lot of crisscross bars," Nancy replied. "Maybe the coat of arms of the old mine owner."

As she climbed down, Bess called from a distance, where she was standing on a little knoll. "I've got a good view of it from here."

George started for the spot when suddenly Bess let out a terrifying scream. Her two friends raced toward her. When they reached the knoll, Bess was trembling with fear.

"What happened?" Nancy demanded.

"Oh, N-Nancy," Bess said, pointing, "I saw a bony hand reach out of the chimney!"

Nancy and George looked. There was no sign of a hand. Bess said she had closed her eyes a moment to shut out the weird sight. When she had opened them again, the hand was gone.

"I think you're goofy," George scoffed. "A person sees things when he gets tired."

"I'm not that tired," Bess retorted. "I saw it. I know I did. I'm getting out of this spooky place."

Wild horses could not hold her. In panic she dashed through the woods toward Nancy's car. There was nothing for the other girls to do but follow her.

Nancy started the motor. Soon they were away from the eerie spot.

"I never want to go there again," Bess declared.

"Not even to help your cousin Dick?" Nancy asked with a grin.

Bess finally conceded maybe she would get over her fright, and she did want Dick to acquire the special clay if possible.

After Nancy left the girls at their homes, she decided to drop into Dick's shop and tell him of her latest discovery. She found a high school boy, who clerked for the young pottery maker after school, behind the counter.

"Would you like something, miss?" he asked.

"I'd like to see Mr. Milton."

"He's busy in the back of the shop right now," the boy answered. "But he'll be through in a minute. Will you wait?"

Nancy smiled. "He's a friend of mine," she said. "I'll go back and see him."

The girl went through the door into the rear room. There she saw Dick engrossed at the potter's wheel, his sandy hair tumbling over his forehead. He was so busy he did not notice his caller.

Nancy watched with rapt interest while Dick deftly pressed a lump of clay on the center of the wheel, then allowed it to rise between his fingers in a spiral column before depressing it again.

Once more the column spiraled. The young

man again pushed it down, at the same time centering and truing the clay. Then he pressed his thumbs into the soft clay, rapidly forming a cylinder.

With one hand inside the cylinder and the other outside, Dick molded the clay into the thickness he desired. Nancy now saw the cylinder shape like magic into a large jar.

Dick snapped off a switch and the whirring wheel slowly stopped. As he turned around, a look of pleased surprise spread over his face.

"Nancy Drew! How did you get here?"

"Simple. That jar you just made is Aladdin's lamp. You rubbed it . . . and I appeared!"

The young proprietor laughed, then grew sober. "I wish we could conjure up a genie to find that China clay pit," he said a bit ruefully.

"Maybe we don't need a genie," said Nancy.

"What do you mean?"

"We may have found the leaning chimney!" Nancy beamed.

Dick gasped. "Honestly? Is there a clay pit near by?"

"I don't know yet." Nancy told Dick what she and her friends had discovered. "I'm going back someday soon to look more thoroughly."

Dick's spirits spiraled like the clay on his potter's wheel. A boyish smile of hope lit his face as he escorted Nancy to the door.

"I'll keep you posted on further developments," Nancy promised.

After dinner that evening she followed her father into his study on the second floor for a chat.

"You're up to something, young lady," he said shrewdly. "What is it?"

Nancy told him of her visit to the strange enclosure. The lawyer frowned.

"I don't like the sound of it," he said. "Strikes me as a good place to stay away from."

"But, Dad!" Nancy protested, her blue eyes growing large with emphasis, "there may be a valuable pit of China clay around there. And if I don't go back, I'll never find out!"

"If it's inside the fence, the owner probably won't want to sell it, anyway," Mr. Drew reminded his daughter. "Well, all right, look around if you wish. But be careful. Don't go there alone."

"All right," she promised.

Carson Drew took a paper from his pocket and said, "I have a clue, too. It's about the Engs."

"What is it?" Nancy asked eagerly.

"I received a phone call from San Francisco this afternoon," Mr. Drew explained, "and my secretary wrote down this report." The tall attorney settled back in his chair and continued:

"It says that when the Engs arrived in San Francisco, on their trip to the United States, they were met at the dock by a man named David Carr."

Nancy quickly went over the name in her mind, but it meant nothing to her.

"Carr was sales representative for the West Coast Trading Company, a San Francisco importing house," the lawyer went on. "He and Eng Moy apparently were acquainted as the result of business dealings. When the Engs left San Francisco on their tour of American pottery plants, Carr went with them."

"What does David Carr look like?" Nancy asked. "Did the report mention that?"

"No," replied Mr. Drew. "The report says there doesn't appear to be any photograph or description of him available. Even the officials of the importing company can't furnish any clues. It seems that Carr did practically all his work for them in China; contacted them by mail. Then, about the time he met the Engs in San Francisco, he dropped out of sight."

"Maybe Carr has something to do with the Engs' disappearance," Nancy speculated.

"Could be," her father agreed. He put the report away. "Anyway, it's a clue to work on."

As Nancy pondered, she glanced idly at a New York City newspaper which lay on her father's desk. Suddenly a small black headline caught her eye. She picked up the paper and scanned the story, then read it to her father.

It described a robbery that had taken place in

New York. An ancient Chinese tea jar, dating from the Sung dynasty, had been stolen off the delivery truck of the Sen-yung Oriental Gift Shop on Madison Avenue.

"Why, that's the place where Mr. Townsend bought the vase for his wife; the one which was stolen during the party!" Nancy exclaimed. "I'll bet there's some connection between the two robberies!"

She decided to put in a long-distance call to the gift shop next morning and find out if the thief had been arrested.

"He may be the same person who stole Mrs. Townsend's vase!" Nancy cried excitedly.

Mr. Drew smiled. "Why not call the New York police tonight?" he suggested. "I'll do it for you if you like."

In a few minutes he had the desired information. The thief was still at large. The lawyer offered a suggestion to Nancy.

"How would you like to go to New York and talk to the owner of the gift shop yourself? You'll get more information that way. Besides, you'll be able to spend a few days with Aunt Eloise."

"It's a deal!" exclaimed Nancy as she hugged her father. She had put off visiting Carson Drew's sister, Miss Eloise Drew, for far too long. "I'll catch the morning plane if I can get a reservation," she decided.

Fortunately, when she telephoned the airport, she was able to get a seat. Then she wired her aunt, telling of her time of arrival.

Packing, although it was for only a two-day trip, took up most of Nancy's evening. She slipped into bed with her head full of pleasant anticipation. New York always held a thrill for her!

Nancy was awakened next morning by a small, cold nose sniffing her hand. She sat up to see Togo, her little fox terrier, squatting on the bed, his eyes fixed on her anxiously. His stubby tail began to wag while he whimpered pleadingly.

"No, Togo," said Nancy with a yawn. "You can't come with me today."

The girl rose and dressed quickly. Two hours later she stepped aboard an air liner and smiled at her father through the window beside her seat while the plane taxied down the field. Then, as it took to the air, Mr. Drew stood waving. As Nancy watched him, he seemed to shrink to the size of an ant.

The trip was smooth and pleasant. In a few hours, the air liner circled for a landing at New York's big airport, then came down.

Nancy peered eagerly for a glimpse of her Aunt Eloise. A moment after the plane landed, she saw her; a tall, attractive woman of middle age. She was smartly dressed in one of the season's newest styled suits.

Miss Drew, whom Nancy strikingly resembled, possessed a charming grace which marked her as a woman of unusual intelligence.

Eloise Drew knew that Nancy was a lot like her, and secretly this gave her a thrill. Years before, when Nancy had lost her mother, Eloise had considered coming to live with her brother. But her girls' school needed her, too, and when Hannah Gruen had proved so satisfactory, she had decided to remain in New York. But Miss Drew enjoyed her niece's visits immensely.

"You look wonderful, Nancy!" she said as they embraced. "And how's your father?"

"He's fine," replied the girl, squeezing her aunt's hand.

"Did you lunch on the plane?" Aunt Eloise asked.

"No."

"Good," said her aunt. "I've made arrangements for lunch at a little garden restaurant in Greenwich Village."

With a porter carrying Nancy's suitcase, they walked arm in arm to a taxi.

The luncheon hour was made particularly exciting by Nancy's tale of the stolen potteries. After the meal was finished, Miss Drew readily fell in with the suggestion that they taxi to Sen-yung's Oriental Gift Shop.

"I know the place," Miss Drew said. "They carry a very fine grade of merchandise."

Some time later their cab swung out of the heavy traffic on Madison Avenue and pulled up before the store. Nancy and her aunt stood outside a moment to admire the many exotic and colorful Chinese potteries and jewelry, and odd pieces of Oriental bric-a-brac displayed behind a large plate-glass window. Then they entered the shop.

Three men, one in deliveryman's uniform, were talking at the rear of the store. One of them came forward as Nancy and her aunt entered.

Nancy hesitated. The name of the proprietor painted on the display window was Chinese, but the man who confronted her was not an Oriental.

"Is Mr. Sen-yung here?" she inquired.

The man shook his head regretfully. "Mr. Sen-yung has been at home ill for the past six weeks," he informed her. "Is there anything I can do for you? I'm Mr. Sen-yung's partner, Mr. Tallow."

"I'm sure you can help." Nancy smiled. "Some time ago Mr. Townsend of River Heights purchased a lovely Ming vase here. I'd like to find out who sold you the vase."

"Mr. Townsend?" the man repeated slowly. "Just a moment. I'll look up the sale in my books."

He went into an office at the rear of the store. As Nancy and her aunt wandered about, examining the beautiful jewelry and porcelain, Nancy could plainly hear the other two men talking. She realized at once that one was a detective. It was evident from their conversation that the deliveryman was the driver of the truck from which the Sung tea jar had been stolen.

"I didn't get a good look at him," she heard the deliveryman say. "I'd just lifted the jar out of the truck to deliver it when I felt a gun at my back. Then a voice told me to get in the truck and drive away."

Nancy stepped up to the two men. She apologized for the interruption and explained her interest in the case. The detective told her to ask as many questions as she wished, but there was little that the deliveryman could add to his story.

"The thief's hat was pulled down and his coat collar turned up," he said flatly. "I was too busy worrying about what he was going to do with the gun to look at him much. I did what he told me to do—left the jar on the sidewalk and scrammed!"

Nancy was disappointed not to learn more. At this moment she felt her aunt's hand on her sleeve.

"Do come look at this vase," Miss Drew urged. "It sounds like the one you were talking about."

She led her niece to a glass cabinet off to one side of the shop. Nancy stared in amazement at the piece on display.   Glazed on jade-green porcelain was a Chinese dragon in black and red.

The same design she had seen woven into the tapestry in Mr. Soong's home!   The one he had said was on his stolen vase!

CHAPTER XI

Pursuit

NANCY hurried to the rear of the shop to find Mr.
Tallow. Before she had a chance to ask about
Mr. Soong's vase, he gave her some startling in-
formation.

"The Townsend vase," he told Nancy, "was sold
to me by a Mr. David Carr."

Nancy stared at him in disbelief. David Carr!
That was the name of the man her father had mentioned; the man who had vanished so mysteriously
in company with the Engs!

"You're quite sure?" she cried.

"Quite." Mr. Tallow smiled pleasantly. "It's
all written down in my ledger."

Nancy pointed out the dragon vase in the case.
"Would you mind telling me where that came
from?" she asked.

"Not at all," Mr. Tallow replied. "I bought
that porcelain only yesterday from Mr. Carr."

Nancy caught her breath. She had been sure

the dragon vase had been stolen from Dick's shop by John Manning. How, then, had David Carr got hold of it?

Were Carr and Manning the same person? Or had Manning sold the vase to Carr, who in turn had sold it to Sen-yung's Oriental Gift Shop? Her brain in a whirl, Nancy turned again to Mr. Tallow in an attempt to find the answers.

"I'm sorry to have to tell you," she said, "but this vase looks just like one that was stolen from a shop in River Heights."

Mr. Tallow's jaw dropped. "It can't be true!"

"The dragon design is exactly the same as the pattern on a Ming vase that belonged to a Mr. Soong," Nancy added.

"Mr. Soong!" the shopkeeper declared. "I know him well! He is an old friend of Mr. Sen-yung! Oh, this is terrible!"

Mr. Tallow looked so worried that Nancy felt sorry for him and asked if she might examine the vase to see if it really were the same one.

"Of course, of course," he agreed.

He unlocked the cabinet door and handed the piece to Nancy. She laid the vase on its side and studied the bottom of it. Clearly painted on the base were several Chinese symbols. They appeared to be exactly like one set of the markings that she had found in Manning's room; the set Mr. Soong had said was on his vase.

Nancy translated the symbols. "Made in the studio of deep peace." She looked at Mr. Tallow. "Is that correct?"

He nodded nervously.

At that moment the door of the shop opened and a short, round-faced Chinese gentleman came in. He took off his hat, exposing a completely bald head, and fanned himself vigorously. Then his mouth spread in a little smile.

"It is hot in the sun," he explained. "Much better to be inside—yes?"

Mr. Tallow hurried toward him. "Mr. Senyung!" he exclaimed. "Thank goodness you're back!"

After introducing his Chinese partner to Nancy, her aunt and the detective, Mr. Tallow repeated what Nancy had said about the dragon vase. Mr. Sen-yung's face became grave. Taking a small magnifying glass from his pocket, he examined the pottery. Suddenly, he straightened with a startled exclamation and turned to his partner.

"When did you buy this vase?" he asked sharply.

"Yesterday," Mr. Tallow replied.

"You should not have bought it without first consulting me!" Mr. Sen-yung told him heatedly.

"But you were ill!" his partner protested. "I didn't want to disturb you!" He looked at the vase, then back at the Chinese. "Is anything wrong?"

"Everything!" Mr. Sen-yung burst out. "This vase is a fake, an imitation!"

Mr. Tallow stared at him, dumfounded.

"How can you tell, Mr. Sen-yung?" Nancy asked.

He showed her the barely perceptible but unmistakable signs that had betrayed the vase to him. Under the magnifying glass the colors showed no signs of having softened with the years, and there was a scent of newness about the porcelain. But most particularly the marks on the bottom stood out a trifle too clearly.

"It is a clever imitation," Mr. Sen-yung admitted. "Extremely expert."

Had this copy of Mr. Soong's vase been made in China and smuggled into the United States by David Carr?

Mr. Sen-yung asked his partner for the complete story of the purchase. Mr. Tallow said he had bought the dragon vase and also the one sold to Mr. Townsend from David Carr. The man had represented himself as a sales representative of the West Coast Trading Company and shown credentials to prove his identity.

Knowing the fine reputation of the San Francisco importing firm, Mr. Tallow had assumed the vases to be authentic. Now it seemed possible that the Townsend vase also was a clever fake.

"We must get the Townsend vase back at once,"

Mr. Sen-yung said. "If it, too, is a reproduction, we'll refund the money."

"It has been stolen," Nancy informed him. "That's really what brought me to New York." Then she asked Mr. Tallow, "What does David Carr look like?"

"He is about medium height," the man replied, "with black hair and dark skin."

"Did you notice his eyes and his shoes?" Nancy asked with rising excitement.

"Not his shoes," Mr. Tallow replied slowly. "At least, I didn't notice anything unusual about them. But his eyes had a peculiar piercing stare."

"John Manning!" Nancy cried.

The two partners, Miss Eloise Drew and the detective looked at Nancy in bewilderment. She quickly told them about the vase thief.

"Don't you see?" she finished. "Manning and Carr are probably the same man!"

"And he's the one who held up the delivery-man!" Mr. Tallow exclaimed. "I just remembered that Carr was here when I gave instructions as to when and where the jar was to be delivered."

"Did Carr say where he's staying?" Nancy asked excitedly.

"No, but I think I know where he may be," Mr. Tallow replied. "He dropped a piece of paper from his pocket. It was a letterhead from the Hotel Royalton."

Asking permission to use the office telephone,

Nancy dialed the Hotel Royalton. David Carr, she was told, was registered at the hotel!

"If we go there now, we may catch him," Nancy declared.

The detective, who had been listening to Nancy's theories with great admiration, led Nancy, her aunt and Mr. Tallow to a police car in front of the store.

Nancy slipped into the front seat with the detective, her suitcase tucked alongside her legs. Eloise Drew and Mr. Tallow climbed into the rear seat. Seconds later, they sped down Madison Avenue.

Swinging west for one block on Forty-second Street, the car swerved south again and raced down Fifth Avenue. As it approached the thirties, the detective slowed down. Then he pulled the car into a side street and braked it to a stop in front of the hotel.

Side by side, Nancy and the detective hurried into the lobby and went up to the desk. The man showed his badge and asked for the number of David Carr's room.

The clerk looked surprised. "Mr. Carr? He just checked out."

Nancy's heart sank.

"But I phoned just a few minutes ago," she protested. "He was registered then."

"I'm sorry," the clerk told her. "He checked out right after you called."

Nancy tried to hide her disappointment. "Did he leave any forwarding address?" she asked hopefully.

The clerk shook his head.

"Mind if we search his room?" the detective asked.

"Go ahead," the clerk replied. He took a key from the rack and gave it to the plain-clothes man. "Room 414."

While Mr. Tallow waited in the lobby, to watch in case the thief should reappear, Nancy, her aunt and the detective took the elevator to the fourth floor. They walked down a corridor to the room Carr had occupied.

The door was ajar. Inside, a maid was cleaning the room. The detective asked to see any scraps of paper she had picked up. The maid showed them to him willingly. He and Nancy pored over the pieces, looking for a possible clue to Carr's whereabouts. But neither the maid's trash bag nor the room itself disclosed the slightest hint.

The detective grunted in disgust. "No use staying here. There isn't a ghost of a clue to where Carr went."

The maid stopped dusting and looked at them. "You mean the gentleman who was occupyin' this room?" she asked.

"Yes," Nancy said hopefully. "Can you tell us anything about him?"

"Well, I can tell you what I overheard," the woman replied dubiously. "Just as I came into the room to clean he was talkin' on the phone. Before he hung up, he said somethin' about meetin' somebody at the Oregon Restaurant."

"Thanks!" cried Nancy.

She ran from the room, followed by her aunt and the detective. A few minutes later they joined Mr. Tallow in the lobby. Then all four drove rapidly toward the restaurant.

The Oregon, a few blocks away, was on a corner. Tingling with eagerness, Nancy almost dragged her aunt into the foyer at the front of the narrow restaurant. The tables, she saw, were arranged along the two walls beyond a row of potted palms.

"Mr. Tallow, see if you can find Mr. Carr," she whispered. "Look through the palms."

Parting the fronds of one of the plants, he obligingly peered at the dining room. Not seeing the suspected thief, Mr. Tallow stepped into the entranceway for a better view.

"There he is!" he called excitedly.

Immediately, there was a commotion at the rear of the room. Nancy saw a man spring from a chair directly in the path of a waiter with a loaded tray. The waiter staggered, then sprawled on the floor, the tray crashing with him. The fugitive raced through the swinging door to the kitchen.

"It was Carr!" Mr. Tallow cried. "I saw him!"

Thrusting the man aside, the detective ran down the aisle between the tables toward the door to the kitchen. Nancy, remembering the restaurant was situated on a corner, darted back toward the front entrance. If Carr should escape through a side door, she reasoned, he would come out around the corner.

Nancy's deduction was right. As she rounded the side of the building, Carr streaked from the restaurant's side entrance. Nancy was on his heels before the detective emerged.

The elusive Carr slipped in and out of the crowd milling on the sidewalk. Pedestrians stared in wonder as Nancy raced after him.

Suddenly she saw Carr dash into a subway entrance. He leaped down the steps three at a time, Nancy after him. Money in hand, he went through the turnstile like a streak of lightning.

Nancy had to pause a moment to get a coin from her bag. Then she went in hot pursuit.

A train stood in the station. Carr ran forward alongside, slipping quickly through an open doorway into one of the forward cars.

In a flash Nancy realized she had no time to reach him. The doors of the train were closing. She leaped inside the nearest car just before the big panel snapped shut. With a lurch, the crowded train started.

CHAPTER XII

The Strange Symbols

NANCY was wedged tightly between the passengers as the train, with a roar, picked up speed in the tunnel under the teeming city.

Reaching for a strap, the girl caught her breath and quickly planned her next move. She *must* push through the crowded train and find David Carr!

She gripped her handbag firmly and started to ease herself among the passengers. Nancy excused herself frequently as she jostled men and women. Finally she reached the end of the car, opened the door and passed into the coach ahead.

Halfway through the car, Nancy was caught by a sudden swaying of the train as it squealed around a curve. Thrown off balance, she careened against the seats and landed directly in the lap of a young man.

"Oh!" cried Nancy, blushing as she struggled up. "I'm *so* sorry!"

"It's all right." The man smiled and helped Nancy to her feet. "I guess you don't live around here! We New Yorkers are used to this!"

Nancy continued her way forward. Finally she arrived at the car into which the suspect had fled. Suddenly it dawned on her that she could not hold him alone. She must have help!

"I'll ask the conductor," Nancy decided, and stood on tiptoe to see if one were in sight.

As she craned her neck, she saw David Carr slouched in a seat near the far door. Near him stood the conductor. Excitedly Nancy moved forward once more.

At that moment the train started to slow for the next stop. In desperation, Nancy forged ahead. Suddenly, with a pitch that threw everybody off balance, the train jerked to an abrupt halt. The doors whipped open. Carr stepped out with the pressing crowd.

"Stop that man!" shouted Nancy. "The dark one with the red tie!"

People around gasped, but no one went after him. Before Nancy herself could get to Carr, he had fled into the sea of humanity milling toward the exit.

When Nancy reached the top of the stairs, David Carr was out of sight. She searched in vain, then, disappointed, hailed a cab. She gave the driver the address of the Oregon Restaurant, where she knew her Aunt Eloise would wait for her.

"Nancy!" cried Miss Drew as the girl stepped from the cab and paid the driver. "Thank goodness you're safe. We feared Carr might have harmed you."

Nancy told her aunt and Mr. Tallow about the chase. As she finished, the detective hurried up to them. He said he had fallen over a stool that Carr had tossed at him in the kitchen of the restaurant. By the time he reached the street, Carr had disappeared. Then he had searched the immediate area to no avail.

All four drove to the police station, where Nancy and Mr. Tallow helped the detective make out a report on Carr. At Nancy's suggestion they telephoned the West Coast Trading Company in San Francisco. As she had suspected, Carr had not been working for them recently.

"Your niece certainly has a good head on her shoulders," the captain said to Miss Eloise Drew, as she and Nancy got ready to leave.

"They say I'm very much like my aunt," Nancy spoke up impishly. "But I'm sorry we didn't catch David Carr."

Reaching the sidewalk, the Drews took a cab to the former teacher's apartment.

Next morning Nancy suggested to her aunt that they tour Chinatown. Recalling that the stolen vases discovered in Masonville had been wrapped in Chinese newspapers, Nancy wanted to go to the office of the *China Daily Times* and make some inquiries.

On the way Nancy and her aunt stopped to admire the many colorful Chinese ornaments displayed in the shopwindows.

When the two sightseers came to Mott Street, they located the newspaper office and went inside. Nancy asked a pleasant man the names of subscribers in Masonville and River Heights. He willingly told her, but neither John Manning nor David Carr was among them.

"Nothing came of that hunch," Nancy told her aunt after they left the office and headed for one of the several fine Chinese restaurants, where delicious, seven-course meals were served.

That afternoon, while they were shopping, Miss Drew remembered that she had a dentist's appointment. She gave Nancy the key to the apartment, saying that she would meet her there. Some time later, as Nancy was finishing a telephone call to the air line's office to reserve plane passage home, she heard the door buzzer.

"Oh, it's Aunt Eloise, I guess," she told herself.

Quickly completing her telephone call, she went to open the door. Suddenly Nancy stopped as she saw a white envelope lying face up on the floor. It had been pushed under the door.

Nancy's own name was scrawled on the envelope in bold letters. Startled, she tore it open. On a plain white piece of paper was printed: "Nancy Drew: Stop work on your case or your life will be in danger!"

The message was unsigned, but Nancy did not have to guess twice as to the probable identity of the sender. Whipping open the door to the hall, she found herself face to face with her aunt!

"What's the matter?" Miss Drew asked. "You look as if you'd seen a ghost!"

"I—I thought maybe I'd find David Carr when I opened the door," Nancy replied.

She showed her aunt the threatening note.

"Why, that explains the strange behavior of the man I saw just as I stepped off the elevator!" Eloise Drew told her niece. "The moment he saw me, he ran down the stairway!"

"Was he dark with piercing eyes?" Nancy asked eagerly as they walked into the living room.

"Yes, I believe he was," her aunt replied. She gave her niece a worried look. "Wouldn't it be wise to give up the case and stay out of Carr's way, dear?" she suggested. "I'm sure he wouldn't have risked delivering that warning unless he's desperate. Apparently he's not going to let anything interfere with his plans—not even your life!"

Nancy patted her aunt's hand reassuringly.

"Don't worry about me, Aunt Eloise," she said.

"I promise to be doubly careful. Anyway, I'm going home, and maybe he'll stay here."

Actually, the young detective felt there was a good possibility, if he were Manning, that he was already on his way back to the River Heights area. She would have to watch her step!

"You're going home?" he aunt repeated. "Oh, Nancy, I thought—"

"Sorry, darling," her niece said, "but a friend of Ned's and mine is being married. Ned's to be an usher. I promised to drive up to Emerson and get him day after tomorrow."

"I hate to have you leave," her aunt said wistfully. "But I bow to the younger generation!"

The following day Nancy boarded the plane for home. She waved to her aunt as she entered the doorway of the air liner, then settled herself comfortably in a seat. On arriving home, she was welcomed by a smiling Hannah Gruen and a barking, tail-wagging Togo.

"Ned Nickerson phoned," Mrs. Gruen told Nancy as she knelt and scratched the terrier's ears. "He said he'd call back."

Ned telephoned again just as Nancy started to unpack.

"Hi!" his voice came over the wire. "Where've you been?"

"New York!" Nancy told him. And she plunged into a quick description of her activities.

"Wow!" he exclaimed when she finished. "You sound like a one-woman police force! Anyway, I'm glad you're back. I'd begun to think you'd forgotten about coming for me."

"Not a chance!" she assured the youth. "I'll be at Emerson tomorrow by twelve o'clock."

"Okay."

Later, Nancy called Mr. Soong. The Chinese gentleman was shocked to hear that an imitation of his rare Ming vase had been sold to the Sen-yung Oriental Gift Shop. He congratulated Nancy on her brave attempt to capture Carr and expressed the hope that the man would be apprehended soon.

Upon reaching Ned's fraternity house next day, Nancy was surrounded by the various members. Having attended many parties there, she was well known and well liked. Though the boys often teased her about her interest in mysteries, there was no one with whom they would rather talk or dance than Nancy Drew.

"Ned's not here," one teased. "Prof kept him after class. How about lunch with me?"

"Say, you big so-and-so," called a youth, clatter-ing down the stairs. "Lay off!"

Ned appeared, grinning, turned Nancy around and marched her back to the car. They had lunch at an attractive inn, then started for Ned's home, a few miles out of River Heights. On the way, Nancy brought him up to date on her latest mystery and her hunt for a China clay pit near the leaning chimney. While they were going through Masonville, she suddenly pulled the car to the curb and stopped.

"What's up?" Ned asked.

They were in front of the courthouse.

"I've been wanting to find out who owns that fenced-in property in the woods," Nancy replied. "Now's my chance. Let's go in to ask the Registrar of Deeds."

Ned followed her up the steps and into the registrar's office. The man handed them a map and ledger. Together they flipped the pages until they came to the entry Nancy was seeking.

Five years before, the record showed, a tract of land comprising some two hundred and fifty acres, including the abandoned Civil War mine, had been purchased by Miles Monroe of Philadelphia.

"Miles Monroe!" Nancy exclaimed in surprise. "That's where he said he came from!"

"Who's he?" Ned inquired.

"A geologist I went to see about the China clay pit. Now I know why Mr. Monroe asked me to let him know if I located it."

"Sounds phony to me," Ned declared. "Want to stop and see him?"

"If you have time."

'I'm not due at the bachelor dinner until seven·

thirty. So let's go. I'd like to see this Mr. Monroe and ask him what he means by trying to put one over on the world's cleverest detective."

"Ned, stop it!" Nancy commanded.

They left the courthouse and drove to Miles Monroe's apartment in River Heights. As before, an eye stared through the peephole in answer to Nancy's ring. When the professor recognized Nancy, the door flew open.

"Glad you called," he said. "I have something to show you. But first, tell me why you came."

Nancy introduced Ned, then quickly got to the problem on her mind. "We've found out your secret, Professor Monroe!"

"My secret?" he asked, perplexed.

"It's you who owns the old iron mine!"

"Me? Well, I'm—!" exclaimed the geologist, his red hair appearing to bristle more than ever. Then he burst out laughing. "I never owned a piece of land in my life!"

"The property is listed as being owned by Miles Monroe of Philadelphia," Nancy told him. "Who could this Miles Monroe be?"

The professor shook his head. "Search me!" he snorted. "To the best of my knowledge I was the only Miles Monroe in Philadelphia."

Nancy felt the man was telling the truth. Since he could tell her nothing more, she put the puzzling question aside for the moment.

"You said you had something to show me?" she reminded him.

The geologist uncrossed his long, bony legs and strode over to the bookcase. He took out a thick volume that looked to be a hundred years old and carefully turned the stained, loose pages to a place he had marked.

"After you told me you were searching for a China clay deposit," the geologist said, "I came across a reference in this old book on geology. It strikes me as the best clue that's turned up yet." He thrust the book abruptly at his young visitor. "Here, read it!"

With Ned looking on, Nancy read the paragraph the professor had marked. It told, in old-fashioned sentences, of a fine white clay that had been found one mile southeast of a "crook in Huntsman's River" during the days of the early settlers.

"Huntsman's River?" Nancy said. "Why, that must be Hunter's Creek. That's the stream which runs under Hunter's Bridge."

"Exactly!" the professor nodded. "And the clay the book describes is China clay, or I'm no geologist!"

"Thank you so much, professor," said Nancy, rising to depart.

Ned shook hands with the geologist. "Nice to meet you, sir," he said. "This sounds like a good clue for Nancy."

When the couple reached the car, Ned suggested that they spend the next afternoon following the directions to the China clay pit.

"And how about Mrs. Gruen packing one of those super lunches of hers?" he added with a grin.

Nancy laughed. "It's a date."

At twelve next day they started out. Nancy told Ned she had learned no Miles Monroe was listed in the Philadelphia directory. Her father had telephoned for the information.

"It's sure a mystery," declared Ned, who was at the wheel this time. "But maybe we'll soon clear it up."

Reaching Hunter's Bridge, Nancy showed him where to park and they locked the car. They stuffed their pockets with the paper-wrapped sandwiches, fruit and thermos bottles of milk Hannah Gruen had prepared. Then they started off, following the water upstream for a mile to a point where it swerved sharply.

"This must be the 'crook' the book mentioned," Ned said. "How about eating?"

Nancy nodded. "And southeast should be in that direction." She squinted at the position of the sun, then pointed to the left.

Ned took a sandwich from his pocket and said "Hurry up!" Nancy bit into one.

Half an hour later the two explorers, their appetites well satisfied, set off once more. When they had gone exactly one mile, as the directions had indicated, Nancy stopped.

"The clay should be near here," she said excitedly.

"Say, what's this?" Ned exclaimed, bending down to examine a little gully. "Do you suppose this is part of the old clay pit?"

The two stepped into the depression, overgrown with weeds and brush. As they did, Ned kicked against a piece of flat, corroded iron.

"Looks as if it's been here a million years," he remarked. "Probably part of an old forge."

"Just what we need!" Nancy cried. "We can use it as a shovel."

"For what?" Ned queried.

"To dig with," the girl said, pointing to the bottom of the gully.

Ned dug. Finally he said ruefully, "Nothing here but a lot of gravel. This isn't a China clay pit. It's only—"

He stopped speaking as a wild cry cut the air some distance ahead. It sounded like *bong*.

"Someone's in trouble!" Nancy exclaimed, starting to run.

A few moments later she and Ned emerged into a clearing. To the girl's utter astonishment, the four-walled enclosure of boards confronted her!

CHAPTER XIII

The Impostor

HAD the cry come from inside the mysterious enclosure?

Nancy ran eagerly toward the fence and listened. There was not a sound.

"How do we get inside?" Ned asked, anxious to help the person in distress.

"There's no opening," Nancy told him. "I wish we could climb over."

"At least we can look over," said Ned, going toward a stout tree limb lying on the ground. It was twelve feet long, four inches thick, and slightly rotted. "If you'll help me, we can prop this against the fence for a ladder, Nancy," he added.

Together they lugged the limb across the clearing and lifted it against the fence.

"You go up while I hold it," Ned suggested.

Nancy placed her hands around the bough and, monkey-fashion, started up the "ladder."

"What do you see?" Ned asked as she reached the top.

"Not much. Trees. Lots of them." She scampered down. "But we're not far from the leaning chimney. Let's go over there and take a look."

Ned willingly dragged the tree limb the short distance and Nancy climbed up again. Below her was a rectangular enclosure, formed on three sides by the fence, and on the fourth partly by a stone wall and the rest by the battered brick building she had seen some days before through a knothole.

Glancing up, Nancy was startled to find that the rusted ornament on the leaning chimney was gone. She looked at the ground below, thinking the symbol had dropped off. It was not there.

"Say, what's so interesting?" Ned called up. "I think I'll look myself."

"Come on up."

Nancy told him about the missing ornament, and also Bess's declaration that she had seen a hand sticking from the chimney. Maybe someone *had* climbed up inside, planning to remove the iron coat of arms, or whatever it was.

"The place gets more mysterious every minute," Nancy remarked.

"It's funny there's no sign of life around, though," Ned commented. "You'd think somebody—"

He stopped speaking as a far-off cry came to

their ears. Again it sounded like *bong*, and again it was impossible to tell whether or not the call of distress had come from inside the enclosure.

Almost simultaneously with the cry came the menacing crack of rotted wood.

"The tree limb!" Nancy cried. But it was too late. Nancy and Ned plunged to the ground!

"You hurt?" Ned asked anxiously, as Nancy did not get up at once.

The girl rubbed her ankle. "This'll be okay in a minute—as soon as I walk a bit."

Ned helped Nancy to her feet. After a few limping steps she declared that her ankle was all right.

"No more sleuthing today," Ned insisted. "Anyway, I can just about make that wedding rehearsal in time. Let's go!"

Nancy hated to leave so soon but said nothing. They trekked back to the car and Nancy dropped Ned off at his home in Mapleton, a suburb of River Heights.

"See you tomorrow afternoon at the wedding," he said, getting out. "And don't let any other usher take you up the aisle!"

Nancy laughingly promised. Then, as she drove on to River Heights, her thoughts turned again to the enclosure in the woods. Both leads which Miles Monroe had given her, the one to the old iron mine and the directions along Hunter's

Creek, had led to the strange spot in the woods.

Was the China clay inside? Did the owner know about it? Nancy set her chin in determination. She would find out! And soon!

Hannah Gruen met her at the rear door of the Drew home, her kindly face lined with worry.

"What's wrong?" Nancy asked quickly.

"Oh, Nancy, Mr. Soong has been phoning you for the past half hour! He's terribly upset!"

"I'll call on him right away," the girl assured her.

"He's not there," Mrs. Gruen told her. "He's at the police station!"

"What for?"

"I don't know," the housekeeper answered, "but I think he's in trouble."

Nancy ran down the porch steps to her car. She drove rapidly, wondering at every turn of the wheels what the police could want with gentle Mr. Soong!

Nancy raced into the station house. The old Chinese gentleman was sitting dejectedly in Captain McGinnis's office. Nancy looked from Mr. Soong to the police officer, then back to Mr. Soong.

"What happened?" she asked.

Mr. Soong, his face lighting at the sight of the girl, opened his mouth to speak. Captain McGinnis intervened quietly.

"Perhaps I'd better explain," he told Nancy.

He picked up a paper from his desk. "I received this report today from the New York City police.

"A woman in New York, named Mrs. Marsden, has complained that a Chinese vase she bought is a fake. She claims it was sold to her by a Mr. Soong of River Heights. She mailed him money orders for five hundred dollars, which he cashed." The officer looked up, adding:

"We've checked with the postal clerk in Mason-ville who paid it. His description of the man who collected the money tallies exactly with that of Mr. Soong."

The Chinese turned despairing eyes on Nancy. "I know nothing about it," he said. "Surely you believe me?"

"Of course!" Nancy said emphatically. "Captain McGinnis, does the report give a description of the vase?"

The officer scanned the paper. "Yes, it does."

The girl quickened with eagerness. She was playing a hunch. If it worked, everything would be straightened out!

"Does it say that the vase is brown," Nancy rushed on, "with a pattern showing an old Chinese sitting beside a deer under a peach tree at the edge of a blue lake?"

Captain McGinnis stared.

"Why, yes!"

"And does it say the Chinese markings on the

bottom of the vase mean 'Made for the hall of fragrant virtue'?"

The police officer's jaw dropped. "How did you know all that?" he demanded.

"Because that vase," Nancy replied evenly, "is the one stolen from the Townsends' home. I saw it there the night it was taken!"

"Well," Captain McGinnis said, "this is a new angle."

"What's more," Nancy continued, "Mr. Soong couldn't have been the thief because I measured the thief's footprints in the flower bed. They were short and wide. And as you can clearly see, Mr. Soong's feet are narrow!"

She paused for breath, and Captain McGinnis wiped his forehead. He sat for a moment, considering, while Nancy watched him anxiously.

"That puts a different complexion on the case," the officer said at last. "But how do you explain the fact that the postal clerk's description of the man who cashed the money orders fits Mr. Soong?"

Nancy deliberated. "The thief probably wore a disguise so he could pass himself off as Mr. Soong," she said finally. "It wouldn't be difficult —a pair of spectacles and a tiny goatee. He must have stolen some means of identification and forged Mr. Soong's signature to the money orders."

"You may possibly be right," the captain said,

"but just the same I think I'll drive Mr. Soong over to Masonville, to see that postal clerk. Want to come, Miss Drew?"

"Yes, indeed."

"We'll go there in my car."

Late that afternoon Nancy, Mr. Soong and the chief arrived at the Masonville post office. At Nancy's suggestion, the two men stayed out of sight while she went up to the money-order window.

Nancy introduced herself to the clerk, then listened carefully as he described the man who had collected the money for the fake vase. His description corresponded exactly with that of Mr. Soong.

"You're quite sure you would recognize the man if you saw him again?" she asked.

"I'm positive!" the clerk told her confidently. "It isn't often that I cash orders for five hundred dollars, so I pay particular attention to anybody collecting that amount of money."

Nancy beckoned to Mr. Soong and had him stand facing the clerk. Chief McGinnis looked on approvingly.

"Is this the man?" she asked.

The clerk stared at the Chinese gentleman.

"That's the one, all right!" he declared. "I'd know him anywhere!"

Nancy thought quickly. There had to be *some* way in which she could prove to the clerk he was mistaken. She took a blank money order from a pile neatly stacked inside the window and gave it to Mr. Soong, together with a pen.

"Please fill it out," she told her friend. Then to the clerk she said, "Perhaps you've overlooked something. Some small detail—"

She broke off as the clerk's eyes widened in watching Mr. Soong write.

"Hey, wait a minute, there is something wrong!" he said. "The Chinese I gave the money to signed his name with his right hand. This gentleman writes with his left hand."

"Then he can't be the same man!" Nancy cried triumphantly.

The clerk shook his head. "No, he can't," he admitted slowly. "In fact," he added, "this man speaks better English. I hadn't thought of that before. But the two of 'em look alike."

Captain McGinnis said he was sorry to have put Mr. Soong in such an embarrassing position. They drove back to River Heights, and Nancy took the elderly Chinese home in her car.

"How can I ever repay you?" Mr. Soong said, stepping to the sidewalk in front of his Colonial house.

"By telling me more someday about your country's beautiful pottery," Nancy said, smiling.

He insisted she come inside at once to be presented with a little gift in token of his gratitude.

As she accompanied the Chinese toward his door, it suddenly swung open. In the entrance stood Mr. Soong's Chinese servant, Ching. His small, inscrutable eyes for once were wide with surprise. Then his lips parted in a toothy smile and he spoke rapidly in Chinese, gesticulating all the while.

Mr. Soong replied in the same tongue. Ching turned to Nancy, his smile growing bigger. Again he spoke the strange language.

"What is he saying?" she asked Mr. Soong.

The old gentleman chuckled. "Ching is thanking you for delivering me from the hands of the police," he explained. "He prays that happiness and good fortune will smile upon you and your family always!"

The servant spoke again and Mr. Soong nodded delightedly.

"Ching is quoting an old Chinese philosopher," he translated. "He says, 'Man roams the world foolishly seeking the rainbow, but the greatest of treasures, friendship, lies in his own garden!'"

"Or to quote an old American proverb," Nancy added, "a friend in need is a friend indeed!"

Mr. Soong chuckled once more. Then he disappeared for a moment, finally returning with a bottle of delicate wisteria perfume imported from China.

"It is little for me to do," he bowed when Nancy thanked him for the gift.

"I'll wear some of it to the wedding I'm going to tomorrow afternoon," she said.

"Miss Tyson's wedding?" the Chinese inquired. "Perhaps I shall see you there."

Mr. Soong was the first person Nancy did see at the church. He arrived just ahead of her. The Oriental was attired in a striking, colorfully embroidered, full-length Chinese ceremonial robe with matching slippers.

"Isn't he a picture?" Nancy murmured to Ned, as he escorted her down the aisle to a pew where Bess and George were already seated.

Then the tall youth left quietly to take up his duties. To Nancy, seeing his fine features over the starched white collar of his dress shirt, he looked more handsome than ever.

Soon afterward the bridal procession walked slowly down the aisle to the strains of the wedding march. The bride, on the arm of her father, was a vision of loveliness in a long, trailing white satin gown and illusion veil.

Bess ohed and ahed, but George whispered, "Hypers, when I get married, it's going to be in a plain tailored suit!"

"Sh!" said Bess.

The ceremony began. Hushed, whispered words. A tender kiss. The triumphal march, with the bride and groom smiling happily as they came down the aisle, then left the church.

Nancy and her friends drove to the reception at the bride's home. After wishing the couple every happiness and having punch and sandwiches, Nancy and Ned went to admire the many lovely wedding gifts displayed in an upstairs room.

Mr. Soong walked in directly behind them. Almost at once, the man's eyes fell on a Chinese porcelain jewel box. He picked it up with a pleased exclamation.

"It's beautiful," said Nancy.

The porcelain jewel case was decorated with plum blossoms. They were painted on a background of deep-blue water lightly coated with cracking ice.

"As you two doubtless know," Mr. Soong said in his soft, musical voice, "most Chinese art tells a story. The plum blossom has been a favorite symbol of our artists for centuries.

"There is a beautiful legend associated with the plum tree that is often used," he said. "A young man, on a pilgrimage to Mount Lo Fou to have his health restored, stopped to rest along the way. Out of nowhere a beautiful woman approached him, perfumed with the delicate fragrance of the plum blossom.

"After conversing with her, the young man fell asleep. When he awoke"—Mr. Soong's eyes twinkled—"he found himself covered with white petals falling like scented snowflakes from a newly grown plum tree beside him. And he was completely cured!"

"What a charming story!" Nancy said.

As Mr. Soong started to replace the jewel box, his eyes suddenly bulged, and he exclaimed something in Chinese.

"What is it?" Nancy asked quickly.

Mr. Soong pointed with a shaking finger to two Chinese symbols worked into the blossoms. They were the same, strange symbols Nancy had seen concealed in the peach-tree pattern on the Townsends' vase!

She turned again to Mr. Soong. The old gentleman's lips were parted. He seemed unable to take his eyes from the symbols.

"What are they?" she asked.

"They are the marks of Eng Moy!" he whispered. "My missing friend, Eng Moy!"

CHAPTER XIV

A Jade Elephant

"ENG MOY!" Nancy gasped.

Mr. Soong nodded slowly, as if he still could not believe it himself.

"I would know my friend's signature anywhere," he declared.

"But I don't understand," Nancy said, bewildered. "If Eng Moy made the jewel box, why didn't he sign his name on the bottom? Why did he work it into the design where it can barely be seen?"

"That I myself do not understand," Mr. Soong told her.

He turned the box bottom up. Several Chinese characters were painted on the base.

"It is from the Wan Li period, the last great epoch of art in the Ming dynasty," the old gentleman informed her. "Eng Moy did not make the vase. Therefore he could not have put his initials on it."

"There's no question that the box is authentic?" Nancy asked suddenly.

"None whatever," Mr. Soong assured her. "Why do you ask?"

Nancy told the Chinese of having seen the two symbols that were Eng Moy's signature concealed in the design of the Townsends' vase. "That piece was an imitation of an old vase," she added.

Mr. Soong stared at the girl in hurt bewilderment. Nancy decided to avoid offending him further by not telling him of a possible link between his friend Eng Moy and the crook David Carr until she had positive proof.

"Perhaps if I learn where this jewel box came from, it will help us find the Engs," she suggested.

Mr. Soong's face lit up. "A splendid idea!" he said enthusiastically.

Nancy wandered about among the wedding guests until she found the bride's mother. Then she asked discreetly if she knew where the attractive old jewel box had come from.

"Why, Mrs. Hunter gave my daughter the box," the hostess said kindly. "It came from that lovely antique shop in Westville."

Nancy knew the store and its proprietor. Only last year she had bought a tea set there for her Aunt Eloise. Nancy made a beeline for the telephone, Ned close behind.

"A swell way to enjoy a reception!" he grumbled in mock disapproval as Nancy dialed the number.

She made a small face at him. "As soon as I finish this call," she promised, "we'll go have some more punch."

"You're on!" he grinned. "And furthermore, we're going from this wedding direct to the Rolling Green Country Club. There's a dance tonight at the club, and some of us from the fraternity have fixed up a little party."

"Fine," Nancy beamed. "Hello? Mrs. Lorimer? This is Nancy Drew of River Heights."

She told the owner of the Westville Antique Shop where she was, then asked about the jewel case.

"Isn't it precious?" the woman effused. "Now let me see— Oh, yes, I purchased that piece several weeks ago from a Mr. David Carr."

David Carr again!

"Was he a man of medium height with rather piercing eyes? Is he from San Francisco?" Nancy asked.

"Why, yes. You know him?"

"I've heard of him. He's a thief, Mrs. Lorimer. If he should show up again, will you please tell the police right away?"

At this instant Bess Marvin rushed up to Nancy. "Come on! Quick!"

Nancy said good-bye to Mrs. Lorimer and hung up.

"Why?" she asked Bess.

"The bride's going to throw her bouquet," the girl said excitedly. "Don't *you* want to catch it?" she asked, glancing sidewise at Ned.

Nancy blushed and rushed away to where eager hands hoped to catch the symbolic "next to be married" bouquet. But she stayed in the background. The maid of honor caught the white roses.

While waiting for the bride to come downstairs, Nancy noticed some guests she had not seen before; Dick Milton and his wife Connie. Going up to them, she learned they had just arrived. Dick had not been able to get away from his shop and Connie had had no one with whom to leave Baby Sue.

"Sue's outside in her carriage," Connie explained, after being introduced.

"It's a shame you missed the wedding," Nancy declared. "Please let me know, Connie, when you want to go out sometime. I'll be glad to come over and stay with Sue."

"That's awfully sweet of you, Nancy. I hate to take you up on it right away, but are you free on the nineteenth?"

"Yes. I'll come over."

"I'd love to go to a luncheon party that day," Connie explained. "Dick's going out of town to see about some different kind of clay."

"Not China clay," Dick spoke up quietly. "You haven't had any luck, Nancy?"

She told him of her recent search and how both of Miles Monroe's clues to the China clay pit had led to the mysterious enclosure in the woods.

"Nothing has come of my trips there yet, but I'm not giving up," Nancy declared. "The first chance I have I'll go out there and do more investigating."

"I hope you'll find the clay," Dick replied, the old worried look returning to his eyes. "The sooner I repay Mr. Soong the better, and there's not much chance of my doing it unless something big comes my way."

"The bride's ready!" an excited girl called out gaily, and paper rose petals were tossed at the bride and groom as they hurried, laughing, down the stairs and through the hall to the front porch. There was the bang of a car door, and the couple were off!

Ned finally found Nancy and, after saying goodbye to their host and hostess, they left for the Rolling Green Country Club with a group of friends. Ned took the wheel of Nancy's car.

"Pretty swell boat, this," he remarked. "Puts my old rattletrap in the shade. Want to sell it?" he teased.

"Not a chance." Nancy laughed. "This car

has shared many mysteries with me. I'd hate to let it go."

Later, when the dance was over, Ned helped Nancy into the car and hopped in behind the wheel to drive home.

"Let's take the Three Bridges Road," she suggested.

"Do you expect to find Manning-Carr at Hunter's Bridge?" he asked teasingly.

"Well, things seem to happen near that bridge," Nancy replied. "He may use it as a place to meet a confederate."

"Okay."

Ned swung the convertible onto Three Bridges Road and drove swiftly toward River Heights. The moon was just coming up. When the car approached the sharp, twisting turns that warned Nancy they were nearing the place where she had encountered the pottery thief, she asked that her companion slow down.

Ned pressed on the brake and coasted. As they slowly rounded the final curve in the series of turns, Nancy stared intently at the underbrush a short distance back from the road. At the spot where she previously had seen a man's telltale footprints, she now saw only the still, black shadows of the night.

Nancy turned her attention to the opposite side of the road, while Ned let the car continue slowly

toward Hunter's Bridge. She fixed her eyes stead-
ily on the grove of saplings that stood several yards
beyond the gradually sloping ground.

In the moonlight the trees stood out like pale,
gray ghosts. Not a creature stirred.

Nancy's glance returned to the road. Suddenly,
behind some bushes at the edge of the creek where
it curved under the bridge, she saw the small white
glow of a flashlight.

"Look!" she whispered excitedly and pointed,
then took her own flashlight from the front compartment of the car. "Stop!" she told Ned. "Let's
investigate!"

Together they got out and stealthily crept down
the embankment toward the light Nancy had seen.
The couple stepped carefully, avoiding twigs and
stones that might make a sound and betray their
presence.

As they neared the shrubs, the light was suddenly extinguished. Nancy and Ned stood for a
moment, hardly daring to breathe, but they
neither saw nor heard anyone.

Finally Nancy beamed her flashlight ahead.
"You sure you saw a light, Nancy?" Ned asked.
"I—Ned!" she cried excitedly.

The next moment Nancy had kicked off her slippers and was wading into the water.

"What—!" Ned exclaimed.

Nancy was soon on the other side of the narrow,

shallow stream.   She swooped up something from the ground and played her light on it.

"What is it?" Ned called.   He was unlacing his own shoes.

She held up the object, a green jade elephant about three inches long and two inches high.

"How'd that get there?" Ned asked.

"Someone just dropped it," Nancy replied, "and I don't believe he meant to."

"I'll come over and help you find him," Ned offered.   "Is the elephant any good?"

As Nancy was about to say she thought it was Mr. Soong's valuable jade piece, there came the roar of a motor.

"My car!" Nancy cried, and ran back across the stream.

Slipping into her shoes, she dashed after Ned, who already was halfway up the embankment. Two feet from the top of the slope they knew the worst.

Nancy's convertible was racing away from them into the night!

CHAPTER XV

A Bold Plan

NANCY and Ned stood aghast as the car's taillight winked smaller and smaller, and finally disappeared.

"Well, if I'm not a nitwit!" Ned said, chagrined. "If I had locked the car this wouldn't have happened."

He knew how fond Nancy was of the speedy convertible and determined to get it back for her quickly.

"We'd better run to a telephone and notify the police," he added. "A state trooper can overtake your car."

Nancy smiled wanly. "I'm afraid we'll be too late, Ned," she replied. "The nearest phone is about two miles from here."

The youth frowned. "I guess our best chance is to thumb a ride," he said at last. "Maybe a car will take us to town in time to do some good."

He looked back at the curve in the road, hoping

a car would appear. But Nancy knew there was small chance of anyone driving through the lonely stretch of woods at that hour. She and Ned started walking toward River Heights, Nancy clutching the jade elephant.

"These aren't exactly hiking clothes," she said with a smile, trying to cheer up her companion.

He looked very forlorn and incongruous in his formal clothes, with a white carnation on his coat lapel. Nancy's high-heeled shoes were not very comfortable on the rough road, and her stockings were still wet from her dash through the creek.

After trudging two miles, the couple came to a gas station, where Nancy telephoned the state police. Listening attentively to her story of the car theft, the officer said he would notify all patrol cars to be on the lookout. Then he promised to send a trooper to take Nancy and Ned to their homes.

Nancy said nothing about the jade elephant, wishing to present it to Mr. Soong or Dick herself.

Not long afterward a car stopped in front of the gas station. Imprinted on its door was the familiar insignia of the state police. Nancy and Ned got into the rear seat, and the car sped toward River Heights.

"Nancy," said Ned, as they reached her house, "I'm due to go back to college early tomorrow morning, but I think I'll stick around here and help hunt for your car."

Nancy would not listen to such an arrangement.

"No, you go on back to Emerson," she insisted. "I have an idea the person who took my car will abandon it somewhere. It'll turn up."

But next morning, soon after Nancy awoke, she learned that the police had not found the convertible abandoned. She went into the dining room where her father was finishing his breakfast of toast and eggs.

"Dad, I'm worried," she announced, seating herself opposite him. "So far the police haven't found a single trace of my car. I guess it's gone for good!"

Togo frisked into the room and barked cheerfully at his mistress. Then he cocked his head at the frown on her face and his stubby tail stopped wagging. Mr. Drew looked thoughtfully at his daughter as she absently scratched the terrier's ears.

"Any idea who took the car?" he asked at last.

"I'm almost certain Manning-Carr or someone he was going to meet is the thief," she answered.

The lawyer took a sip of coffee. "You're probably right," he agreed. "And I don't like the situation at all. I've done some more checking on Carr."

"Tell me about him," Nancy said, regaining her enthusiasm.

"I found out from the authorities in Washington," Mr. Drew went on, "that he's wanted for smuggling and a dozen other offenses. Seems he's of mixed blood."

"Part Chinese?" Nancy interrupted.

"Exactly," the attorney replied. "His mother was Chinese. He's American on his father's side. In appearance, Carr is supposed to resemble his father."

"Oh!" Nancy said excitedly. "Now I'm beginning to put two and two together."

"And that's not all the story," said her father. "Carr has a brother who's also reported to be a criminal. But he's too smart for anything definite to be known about him. He may be in the Orient or he may be in the United States; the authorities aren't sure which."

"Does he look like Carr?" Nancy asked quickly.

"No," the lawyer replied, "he looks like a Chinese."

Nancy let her thoughts ramble over this information. She was sure now the brother was working with Carr. That would account for the other set of footprints which had baffled her. It also would account for the person who had cashed the money orders made out to Mr. Soong.

"Carr's brother may be hiding in the enclosure in the woods," she said to herself after her father had left the house. "Even Carr may be there!"

Nancy determined that as soon as she found out

if the jade elephant really were Mr. Soong's she would investigate the enclosure. She would ask if Bess or George could use the family automobile and drive her out there. This time she was going to find out why the fence had been built!

Hannah Gruen insisted upon knowing what Nancy was planning. She thought it might be dangerous and felt it was her duty to warn Nancy.

"You may be trespassing on property that doesn't concern you or the mystery," she pointed out. "Innocent people may live there, and they would have a perfect right to guard their property from intrusion."

Nancy hugged the faithful housekeeper. "If something happens to me, I know you'll come to the rescue!"

As Nancy walked to the telephone, Mrs. Gruen smiled. She knew that the young detective was determined to solve the mystery, but that she would not do anything foolhardy.

Mr. Soong did not answer his telephone, so Nancy dialed Dick Milton's shop.

"Hold everything, Dick!" she said. "I believe I've found the stolen jade elephant."

"No fooling?"

Nancy described the piece.

"That's it, all right!" Dick exclaimed excitedly.

She asked him if he wanted to return the article to Mr. Soong personally.

"It'll be much safer at your house," he declared. "Anyway, you found the elephant. Please take it to Mr. Soong."

Nancy agreed and carefully concealed the piece in a drawer of the dressing table in her bedroom. She would carry the jade piece to its owner later.

Humming cheerfully at the prospect of finding the key to the mystery of the enclosure in the woods, Nancy set out for Bess Marvin's house. She saw her plump, blonde friend putting golf balls with George on the lawn. Nancy watched as George stroked the ball and missed the cup by a wide margin.

"Nice shot," she observed.

George looked up. "Hypers!" she exclaimed. "When did you arrive?" She glanced at the curb and her eyes opened wide. "Where's your car?"

Nancy described the events of the night before and the girls listened with increasing astonishment.

"So I'm looking for a driver to take me to the mystery enclosure," she said in conclusion.

"Again?" gasped Bess. "I don't like that place."

"Oh, don't be a ninny," George retorted. "Nothing awful happened to us the last time we were there."

"All right," Bess agreed reluctantly. "I'll ask mother if we can take the car."

After a few minutes she reappeared with the

information she could have it later, and it was four o'clock when they started off. This time they tied a ladder to the top of the car.

Bess headed for Three Bridges Road. Then she turned onto the gravel road and a short time later Bess parked the car and the three girls started off through the woods, carrying the ladder.

When they finally emerged from the trees and saw the familiar four-walled wooden enclosure in the clearing before them, they paused to rest. The mysterious compound was as strangely silent as ever, and even the surrounding forest seemed eerily still.

Bess looked apprehensive. "Oh, Nancy, I don't like it!" she whispered. "I feel as if ghosts were hiding behind every tree. Let's go back!"

"Don't be a loon!" George scolded her cousin. "There's not the slightest indication of a ghost."

"But that hand in the chimney . . ."

"Wasn't there," George declared.

Bess subsided uncomfortably, with nervous glances at the surrounding area. Nancy and George picked up the ladder and the three girls walked on. Passing the knoll near the location of the leaning chimney, Nancy decided to take a look from there.

"Bess, maybe you were right!" Nancy cried. "Maybe someone *did* reach a hand out of the chimney! There's a new symbol up there now!"

The cousins rushed to Nancy's side and stared in amazement. Nancy, puzzled, told them that the original iron ornament was missing when she and Ned had looked at the chimney.

"This new one," she said, taking a pencil and pad from her purse, "is like the other one, only it has more crosspieces."

"Looks like an Oriental character of some sort," George remarked.

"Yes," said Bess. "Maybe some Orientals live here." The thought somehow made her feel better. At least the inhabitants were not ghosts!

Nancy said nothing. She asked the others to help her prop the ladder against the fence, then nimbly climbed it.

The scene inside the enclosure was exactly the same as when she had viewed it with Ned. There was little to be seen because of trees and bushes.

Climbing down, Nancy suggested they move the ladder to a part of the fence over which she had not looked before. The girls carried it to the end of the enclosure opposite the leaning chimney.

Once more Nancy looked into the grounds. And once more she was disappointed. Trees, and more trees.

"See anything?" George demanded.

Nancy glanced down at the girl and shook her head.

"There's not a sign of any living creature," she reported.

"Maybe people just come here once in a while," George ventured.

"They go in and out all right," Nancy said, and added excitedly, "Girls, I see the entrance gate!"

"Where?" George demanded.

"Not far from where I'm standing. It's very cleverly constructed so it doesn't show from the outside."

She had barely uttered this statement, when Nancy's attention became fixed.

"Someone's coming!" she announced. "A strange-looking person!"

CHAPTER XVI

The Threat

COMING toward Nancy among the trees of the wooden enclosure was a tall woman dressed in a flowing lavender robe. Over her head she wore a faded hood of the same color. Encircling her waist was a knotted rope, the ends of which dangled as far down as her sandaled feet. She stared at the girl perched on the ladder.

"Get down from there at once!" she ordered. "Go away and never return!"

Going to the gate, she lifted the iron latch and pulled the cleverly concealed gate open. Nancy scrambled down the ladder, as the woman appeared outside the fence and came rapidly toward the three girls.

"What are you doing here?" she demanded, her face flushing angrily.

Bess gulped. So harsh and intense was the woman's attitude that the girl was more than a bit frightened.

"We didn't mean any harm—" Bess started to stammer, but Nancy interrupted her.

"We're searching for something," she explained to the woman with a friendly smile. "We were looking to see if it might be on the other side of the fence."

"You have no right to spy on our grounds!" the woman retorted sharply. "Go away now, and don't come back!"

Bess tugged at Nancy's sleeve. "Come on, Nancy!" she whispered pleadingly. "We'll only make her angrier if we stay!"

Nancy ignored her friend's suggestion.

"We'll leave as soon as we learn what we came to find out," she said.

The woman's eyes narrowed. "What do you want to know?" she asked after a moment.

"We're searching for a pit of China clay," Nancy told her. "We have reason to believe it's in this vicinity. Can you tell us anything about it?"

The woman's hands clenched below the long, wide sleeves of her robe.

"I know nothing of such a thing. Heed my warning and never come back!"

George, who had been staring at her long, hooded robe, asked suddenly, "Are you a member of a religious sect?"

"I belong to the Lavender Sisters," the woman replied. "We have contacts with few."   She pointed to the wooden partition. "The gardens beyond that wall are sacred. Those who dare defy us and trespass will be tortured by evil spirits to the day they die!"

"Evil spirits!" Bess gasped.

The woman looked skyward, then she stepped closer to the three girls and lowered her voice to a hushed whisper.

"These gardens are our heavens," she intoned. "We gather inspiration in the trees and the flowers! We Lavender Sisters have made these grounds our home; a shrine where only the true believers may worship in privacy and peace! Begone, and do not disturb us again!"

"We won't!" Bess promised hurriedly.

She turned to Nancy appealingly, but the young detective was not yet ready to go.

"Do Oriental women live here with you?" she inquired.

The Lavender Sister gave Nancy a searching look. "No. Why do you ask?"

"Because of the symbol on the chimney," Nancy replied.

"The symbol?" the woman asked, puzzled. Then she added quickly, "Oh, yes, the symbol. I had forgotten."

She gave no further explanation, and again ordered the girls away.

"Help me carry the ladder, George," Nancy said.

The two girls removed it from the fence. With Nancy carrying one end of the ladder and George the other, the friends started back through the woods. The woman watched them until they were out of sight, then she quickly re-entered the wooden enclosure and latched the gate behind her.

"What a strange place for a religious colony," Bess said, ducking under a low-hanging branch.

"I'm not convinced it *is* a real religious colony," Nancy replied.

"Me neither!" George declared. "Most of the things the woman said sounded like a lot of mumbo jumbo! I think she's funny in the head."

"You can't tell," Bess observed seriously. "Her clothes were like those of some religious groups. And she said the ground inside that old fence was sacred ground. Anyway," she added with an air of finality, "I'm just as glad we're going away from the place. I don't want any part of evil spirits!"

"Say!" George exclaimed when they reached a dirt lane, "this isn't the way we came, but maybe it connects with the gravel road."

They had gone about two hundred feet when Nancy, who was walking somewhat ahead of the others, stopped short, with the result that George, who was toting the rear end of the ladder, nearly lost her balance. And a moment later, Bess, bringing up the rear of the procession, bumped solidly into her cousin.

"Hey!" George cried indignantly. "Why don't you tell a—"

Her voice trailed off as she saw Nancy staring fixedly at something directly ahead of them in a small clearing!

It was Nancy's car!

"Hypers!" George cried in disbelief.

The girls dropped the ladder and rushed forward. The convertible was quite undamaged. Even the license plates were the same.

"The thief probably hasn't had a chance to substitute new plates," Nancy told the others.

She opened the door and looked inside the car. Everything was just as she had left it, but the ignition switch was locked and the keys were missing. On the floor, however, lay an old pair of height-increasing shoes.

"Oh!" cried Bess.

Nancy turned and faced her friends.

"I don't know about you two," she declared, "but I'm going back to the enclosure and get inside! It's no coincidence that we've found my car and these shoes here. I'm sure the car was stolen by some friend of Manning-Carr, and I'll bet that enclosure is their hide-out."

"That's why the Lavender Sister didn't want us around," George added. "I'll go back with you, Nancy, and see what we can find out."

"But we mustn't get caught," Bess warned.

"That woman—maybe Carr—and those evil spirits—"

She glanced around apprehensively at the woods, then at the narrow, winding lane. She did not want to stay near the car alone; she did not want to run into danger by going back. Finally, helpless and defeated, she said:

"I'll go, too."

The sunlight was hidden by a sudden overcast when the girls again emerged from among the trees and went toward the fence. Nancy placed the ladder in a different spot from where she had put it before and quickly climbed to the top.

"Keep watch!" she whispered. "I'll come out the gate."

It was but the work of a moment to break the rusted strands of barbed wire. Then, taking a final look around to make doubly certain she was unobserved, the young sleuth let herself down inside the enclosure.

She crept cautiously to the edge of a clearing. To the right was the stone wall and the front of the old brick building with the leaning chimney.

Hardly had Nancy decided to leave the concealment of the shrubs, when she saw the Lavender Sister suddenly come through a small wooden door in the stone wall. At her side trotted a huge mastiff!

Nancy drew back farther into the fringe of

bushes, hoping that her movements would go undetected in the failing light. The huge dog raised his head as if listening but did not look in her direction.

The woman headed with the mastiff toward the gate in the fence. As they came closer to Nancy, she saw that the dog was held in leash by a long, thin steel chain attached to his collar.

Nancy watched with sudden apprehension as the woman went up to the gate. Suppose she should leave the enclosure? She would surely see Bess and George waiting outside!

But luck favored the girls. Stepping to one side of the gate, the Lavender Sister hooked the thin steel leash to an iron ring attached to one of the boards. Leaving the mastiff to stand watch, she started back toward the brick building.

So relieved was Nancy at her friends' escape from detection, she had not for the moment realized her own plight. But as her eyes returned to the mastiff, the truth struck her with sickening force.

She could neither do any investigating without attracting the dog's attention, nor could she leave the wooden enclosure by way of the gate!

Indeed, she dared not make the slightest sign or sound that would betray her presence to the mastiff and set him to baying an alarm.

She was trapped!

CHAPTER XVII

A Mad Dash

NANCY felt a wave of panic, but she swiftly steeled her nerves. Now was the time for cool, analytical reasoning, she told herself firmly; not a surrender to sudden fears.

"If I go in the other direction, away from the dog, maybe he won't detect me," she decided. "I'll worry later about getting out of here."

Nancy tiptoed along, making her way to the old brick building. Not a sound could be heard from within. She tried the door. It was locked.

Suddenly lights sprang up behind some distant trees and spread a low white glow over the area. A moment later a red glare flared up briefly and Nancy could hear indistinct voices.

Presently there was a clink of metal, the rattle of a chain. Then an engine sputtered, coughed and finally settled down to a steady, monotonous chug-chug-chug.

"What's that for?" Nancy wondered. "It might be a water pump, but why all the lights?"

Starting forward, she suddenly found her path blocked. Two Lavender Sisters came out of the shadows. One stood as if guarding the unseen operation. The other walked briskly toward the mastiff. Nancy recognized her as the woman she, Bess and George had encountered earlier.

The dog rose at her approach, and the woman placed a large tin pan heaped with raw meat in front of him. As the dog's jaws crunched into the meat, the Lavender Sister turned to go back. At this moment in a low but clearly audible voice from outside the high board fence came a call.

"Nancy!"

It was Bess's voice!

She called again, even more anxiously. "Nancy! Where are you?"

Nancy longed to reply, but more fervently than that she wished Bess would stop calling, because the woman had stopped and was staring in the direction of the voice.

Hastily Nancy tiptoed nearer the fence. Taking a notebook from her bag, she quickly scribbled a warning:

"Hide!"

She tore off the page, wadded it into a small paper ball and tossed it over the fence. She hoped

Bess or George would see it. Then she looked again toward the woman.

The Lavender Sister seemed to be hesitating, not certain whether to investigate or not. Then with sudden decision she walked toward the gate and pushed up the latch.

"The ladder!" Nancy remembered wildly.

What if the girls had left it propped against the fence and the woman instigated a search of the grounds to see who had climbed over!

As the long-robed figure slipped outside the wooden enclosure, Nancy waited with bated breath for the outcome of the woman's search. Seconds dragged into minutes, but there was no sound. Finally, the Lavender Sister reappeared inside the grounds and shut the gate behind her.

Nancy drew a sigh of relief. Apparently, the girls had hidden in the near-by woods, taking the ladder with them.

Nancy's hope of seeing more of the grounds to learn if there were a China clay pit within them, or to locate Manning-Carr or his brother, faded as time went on. The two Lavender Sisters stood in stony silence, barring all chance to do this. Finally, Nancy concluded she would have to give up and try to get out of the place.

"But that awful beast!" she told herself.

The mastiff uttered a low, throaty growl as if

he sensed an alien presence. Nancy scribbled a second note to Bess and George, briefly describing her plight. After tossing it over the fence, she waited for a reply.

But no reply was sent. Neither a similarly wadded note nor the sound of a voice came over the top of the wooden partition.

Nancy was worried. Had the two girls gone off and left her?

"They'd never do that," she thought. "I hope they didn't run into any trouble."

This thought spurred her on to seek an escape from the enclosure and find out what had happened to them.

The dog stretched himself on the ground beside the gate, his massive head resting quietly but watchfully between his paws. Nancy looked at him and bit her lip in vexation.

"Guess there's only one thing to do," she reflected. "That's to wait until somebody comes and takes the brute away."

An hour passed, the girl hoping against hope. But apparently the dog had been stationed beside the gate for the night.

A bold plan half formed in her mind, and she searched the ground along the fence until she found a rock beneath a shrub. Nancy folded her fingers around it experimentally, then slipped the rock into her bag.

"It's dark enough now for me to try my experiment," she decided.

She stole stealthily among the trees and bushes in the direction of the dog. When about fifty feet from him, she stopped and took stock of her position. The ground that separated her from the dog was bare.

She took the small rock from her bag and weighed it in her hand. Then she carefully approximated the length of the dog's thin steel leash.

"Here's hoping!" she murmured, aiming at an imaginary spot on the fence several yards beyond the animal.

Slowly drawing back her arm, Nancy let the rock fly with unerring accuracy. The mastiff bounded to his feet as the rock struck the boards with a loud noise and ricocheted into some bushes. He stared at the spot and bared his teeth in a low growl. Then he trotted alertly toward the fence and nosed among the foliage.

Nancy stood poised on the balls of her feet, waiting until the dog had gone as far from the gate as his leash would permit. Then she darted forward, lifted the latch and tugged at the gate.

The mastiff heard her and raced back with a fierce snarl. For a frightening instant, Nancy thought the gate would never open. Then it swung in, and she raced outside the enclosure a split second ahead of the dog!

Glancing over her shoulder, Nancy saw the dog lunge and paw the air as he came to the end of his leash. A moment later angry barks filled the night. As the girl dashed among the trees, she heard excited women's voices from the enclosure.

"Oh, I hope they don't let that beast loose!" Nancy said fervently.

In the darkness she could not at once determine the direction she should take but dared not pause.

"I *must* get away!" she told herself.

Running as rapidly as she could in the darkness, ducking under low-hanging branches, dodging around bushes, she suddenly stumbled onto a narrow dirt lane. It appeared to be the same one Nancy and the two cousins had found that afternoon. Assuming it must lead to the gravel road, Nancy followed the path thankfully.

But her relief was short-lived! Bright white beams of light began to flash among the trees a distance behind her.

Her pursuers had picked up her trail! With the advantage of light, they began to gain on her. Her breath coming fast, Nancy went on around a bend in the lane. She stopped short.

Coming toward her along the winding path was a car. Its lights blinded her temporarily. The driver surely had seen her. Now there certainly was no chance to escape!

Suddenly a wild thought came to Nancy.

Maybe this was unexpected aid!   Perhaps the girls had fled from the mysterious woods to summon help.

Nancy stared at the car tensely.   With a gentle squeal of brakes, it rolled to a stop.   Its lights dimmed.

Was she to be rescued or captured?

CHAPTER XVIII

A Burglar

NANCY stood frozen to the spot. Not a sound permeated the woods from the direction of the car.

The next thing Nancy heard, from somewhere behind her, was a woman's clear-cut voice. "That dog must have opened the gate," she said excitedly. "You know he did it once before. We may as well go back."

Nancy was jubilant. The Lavender Sisters did not know she had been inside the enclosure! But there was still uncertainty ahead. Courageously the girl stood her ground to see what would happen down the lane. A moment later a small figure bounded out of the darkness and wagged its tail joyously.

"Togo!" Nancy exclaimed.

Her tension gave way to relief, and she hurried forward. In a few moments she was joined by Bess, George, Dick Milton and Hannah Gruen.

"Nancy! Nancy, are you all right?" the Drew housekeeper whispered hoarsely.

She stopped breathlessly in front of the girl and hugged her.

"Yes, I'm all right," Nancy replied. "But I'm certainly glad to see you."

"Hypers!" said George. "You scared Bess and me silly."

"Yes. What happened?" Bess demanded.

Nancy glanced swiftly over her shoulder. There were no further signs of pursuit. Apparently the mysterious women had abandoned the chase.

Nancy told her story. She ended by telling Dick that despite her efforts she had learned nothing new about the China clay pit.

"The important thing is that you're safe," Hannah Gruen declared. "Now let's get out of here. Nancy, I wish mysteries could be solved without your taking such chances! I'm sure your father will be terribly upset when he hears about this!"

"Where is Dad?" Nancy asked. She had wondered at her father's absence from the rescue party.

"He received an urgent telephone call from Washington," Mrs. Gruen explained. "I packed a few things for him and he caught the afternoon plane. He said to tell you he didn't know how long he'd be gone; that he'd return as soon as possible."

Nancy nodded. She wondered if the lawyer's trip to Washington concerned the Engs. Her thoughts were interrupted by Bess.

"George and I couldn't imagine what in the world had happened to you in that enclosure," she said, as they walked toward her car. "We waited and waited for you to come back. When you didn't answer after I called, well, George was all for going inside to find you! Then your note came over the fence, and we didn't know what to think!"

"But we hid in the woods anyway," George supplied, "just as you warned us to."

"And not a second too soon, I can tell you!" Bess went on. "We'd hardly jumped behind a tree when that Lavender Sister came outside and stared exactly at the spot where we'd been waiting!"

"What about the ladder?" Nancy queried, still curious. "Couldn't she see it?"

"It wasn't there," George informed her. "We took the ladder away from the fence right after you let yourself down inside. We hid it under a bush at the edge of the woods, since you said you were coming out the gate."

"When that woman appeared," Bess took up the story, "we saw that awful mastiff chained right inside the gate." The girl gave a slight shudder. "So we knew you *couldn't* get out!"

After the Lavender Sister had re-entered the enclosure, the cousins explained, they had hurried through the woods to Bess's car and driven to Nancy's home to get her father. Learning the lawyer had left for Washington, Bess had telephoned Dick Milton and asked him to return with them. Hannah Gruen, upset and anxious, had announced that she and Togo would go along too.

"It's a good thing we found the lane this afternoon," George declared, "or we couldn't have got here so fast."

"And a good thing I took it," Nancy said ruefully, "or you'd have missed me!"

They got into Bess's car and drove off. As it curved around another bend in the winding dirt lane, the headlights focused on Nancy's convertible, still parked in the small clearing. Mrs. Gruen had brought the spare key to the ignition switch and, after a moment's hesitation, she gave it to Nancy.

"Are you sure you feel well enough to drive?" she inquired anxiously.

"You bet I do!" Nancy smiled at her. "Just being able to drive my car again gives me a lift!"

Easing into the driver's seat, she turned on the motor and listened to its sound with evident satisfaction. Mrs. Gruen climbed in beside the girl and, whistling to Togo to join them, Nancy put the car in gear and followed Bess toward home.

They drove slowly over the narrow lane until they arrived at the gravel road. Then the two drivers speeded up and were glad when the roofs of River Heights came into view. Nancy pulled up at a corner a few blocks from where Bess lived. Bess stopped her car alongside and called across:

"Think you can get home safely without us to watch over you?"

Nancy laughed. "I guess I can manage!" she replied. "You've done your good deed for tonight. Thanks a million."

She waved, then drove straight on while Bess turned off toward Dick's home. A few minutes later Nancy came to her own street and swung the car into the driveway of the large, comfortable Drew home, which stood some distance back from the street.

"That's strange!" Mrs. Gruen spoke up in amazement. "I left the lights on in the living room and hall when I went out."

Nancy's eyes followed her glance. The windows were completely dark. Suddenly the terrier began to bark excitedly.

"What is it, Togo?" Nancy asked quickly.

She opened the door of the car and the dog jumped out. He dashed up the front steps and scratched at the door.

"He acts as if someone were in the house!" Mrs. Gruen exclaimed.

Nancy nodded. "Go around to tne back of the house," she instructed Mrs. Gruen. "I'll take the front entrance. If there *is* a burglar inside, maybe we can trap him."

"All right," the woman agreed. "But be careful, Nancy."

"I will," the girl promised. "And you too."

She waited until the housekeeper got to the rear yard, then she went up the front steps.

Togo barked as she set foot on the porch. Turning her key in the lock, Nancy opened the door, snapped on the hall light, and looked inside. Togo sniffed the floor, racing from one room to another. No one was around, and apparently nothing had been disturbed.

Stealthy footsteps approached from the rear of the house and Nancy was joined by Mrs. Gruen. "I didn't see a soul—" the housekeeper began in a whisper, then broke off as Nancy's finger tightened on her arm.

From the second floor of the house had come a soft distinct sound!

"Come on!" Nancy whispered.

She flicked a switch to turn on the upper hall lights, then cautiously ascended the stairs, followed by Mrs. Gruen. Togo went ahead of them.

Nancy had just snapped on a light in her own bedroom when the dog began to bark wildly down the hall. As she turned to go after him, she glanced at her dressing table. The drawer had been lifted out and its contents strewn on the floor! One look told Nancy that Mr. Soong's jade elephant, which she had not had time to deliver, was gone!

"That's what the thief was after!" Nancy thought excitedly.

She turned to search the other rooms for the intruder when a scream came from a back bedroom.

"Help! Help!"

CHAPTER XIX

Mistaken Identity

RECOGNIZING the distressed voice as Mrs. Gruen's, Nancy ran to the back room. She found the house-keeper unhurt but staring wildly out the window.

"He went that way!" she cried, pointing toward the garden. "He jumped off the back porch roof and disappeared over the hedge!"

Nancy raced downstairs with Togo in pursuit of the burglar. But her chase was fruitless. He had too much of a head start. Upon her return she asked the housekeeper what the man looked like.

"I'm afraid I didn't get a good look, Nancy," Mrs. Gruen confessed. "It happened so fast, all I could think of was to call for help!"

They searched the house. Nothing but the jade elephant was missing, but desk, closet and dresser drawers had been searched, as evidenced by their disarray.

Nancy stood lost in thought. The man was no

ordinary burglar or he would have stolen other things; silverware, jewelry, valuable pieces of bric-a-brac, of which there were many in the Drew home.

Who could the thief be? Manning-Carr?

Accompanied by Mrs. Gruen and Togo, Nancy went outside with a flashlight and examined the soft earth at the back porch.

She soon found the footprints she was seeking, deeply imbedded in the ground from the force of the thief's jump. They looked like the same short, wide prints she had seen in the Townsends' flower bed after their vase had been stolen!

"I feel kind of fidgety," Mrs. Gruen remarked after they had returned to the house and made sure all the doors and windows were locked for the night.

Nancy called the police. She reported that she had recovered her car, then told of the theft of the jade elephant. As a routine matter they came and made an investigation. Then the girl had a snack and wearily tumbled into bed.

Her waking thought was of Mr. Soong and she determined to go to his home at once to talk to him. Not only did she have the unpleasant task of telling him about the jade elephant, but she was eager to learn from him the meaning of the strange Oriental symbol on the leaning chimney.

As on previous visits, the door to Mr. Soong's

house was opened by Ching, the servant. His expressionless face spread into a smile as he saw the girl and he made a deep bow.

"Is Mr. Soong at home?" Nancy asked.

A look of regret quickly replaced the man's smile and he shook his head, then spoke rapidly in Chinese. Nancy listened without understanding.

"Not at home?" she finally inquired, shaking her head to make herself understood.

Ching nodded a few times and made a sign with his hand to show that his master had gone out. Nancy deliberated a moment, then took a notebook from her purse and scribbled a short message to call her at the house or after twelve-thirty at Dick Milton's home. This was the nineteenth, and she had promised to take care of Baby Sue. Nancy tore off the page, folded it in half and wrote Mr. Soong's name on it.

She gave the message to Ching and he gesticulatingly promised to deliver it. Then he bowed smilingly and closed the door.

Nancy went back home to await Mr. Soong's call. But though the telephone rang several times, none of the callers proved to be Mr. Soong.

"Oh, dear, I hope he hasn't gone out of town," she sighed, then snapped to attention as the instrument rang again.

This time a new kind of surprise awaited her.

"Nancy Drew?" a voice boomed. "Come **right over** here!"

"Is this Mr. Monroe?" she asked.

"Sure is. And I believe I have a clue to **the** China clay pit to show you."

"What is it?"

The geologist refused to impart any further information over the telephone. Grabbing **her** purse, Nancy explained her errand to Hannah Gruen, then ran from the house and hopped **into** her car.

This time the tall, sharp-featured professor answered her ring immediately, without first resorting to the peephole. He led Nancy into the living room in silence. Taking a package from his desk, he thrust it into her hands.

"What do you make of this?" he barked.

Nancy looked at the package. It had been **sent** by parcel post from San Francisco and had obviously been unwrapped. Its strong cord now **was** tied around it loosely.

She studied the address. Painted in bold, **black** letters on gray paper were the words:

M. Monroe
General Delivery
River Heights

Nancy looked questioningly at the geologist. "Open it!" he commanded.

She untied the cord and opened a white cardboard box inside the paper. Neatly packed in rows were several tubes of paint with Chinese markings.

"This is the kind of paint potters use!" Nancy exclaimed in surprise as she recalled similar tubes of paint at Dick Milton's workshop.

"It is!" Professor Monroe snorted. "And these tubes must have been shipped from China. Their colors are among the finest and purest I've seen! Only thing is," he added dramatically, "I didn't order them!"

"Who did then?" Nancy asked.

"I'll let you guess," the geologist answered, grinning.

Nancy glanced again at the address on the wrapping paper. "This package must have been meant for the other Miles Monroe!" she cried. "The man who owns the tract of land near Hunter's Creek!"

"Precisely!" the professor boomed, and his eyes sparkled. "And why would our mysterious friend have the paints sent to him unless he intended to use them on porcelain?"

Rising excitement tingled inside Nancy. Now she was convinced that the strange, fenced-in enclosure was near a pit of China clay. And someone was making pottery there!

"I'll take the package back to the post office,"

she told the geologist, "and stand watch until Mr. M. Monroe calls for it!"

"Good idea!" he barked. "Go to it!"

To herself Nancy said, "And I'll bet this other M. Monroe is Manning-Carr. Oh, dear, I wish I hadn't promised Connie Milton I'd take care of Sue today. There's no time to lose on this mystery."

But Nancy was a person of her word, and she would not disappoint Connie. She did decide, however, to call first Bess, then George, to ask them to help her out if something vital should develop. Using the geologist's telephone, she called but was told that both girls would be away until late afternoon.

"So I'm on my own this time," Nancy reflected, leaving the geologist's apartment.

When she arrived at the General Delivery window of the post office, she met with both disappointment and a surprise.

"That package for M. Monroe was called for only fifteen minutes ago!" the clerk informed the girl as she handed him the parcel and explained the error. "Mr. Monroe was plenty angry when I told him I gave it to the professor!"

Nancy's hopes sank.

"Is Mr. Monroe a dark-skinned man with black hair and piercing black eyes?" she asked, giving the clerk a description of Manning-Carr.

The clerk shook his head decisively.

"The man I talked to," he said, "was Chinese."

"Chinese!" she exclaimed. "Are you sure?"

"Sure I'm sure!" the clerk retorted. "I guess I can tell a Chinese when I see one!"

"What did he look like?" Nancy persisted.

The clerk stared at her helplessly. "Why, uh— like a Chinaman!" he replied.

Nancy bit her lip in vexation. "But can't you remember anything special about him?" she asked. "Any distinguishing features, such as the shape of his nose, the color of his eyes, or the way he talked—"

"Listen, miss," the clerk cut in impatiently, "I'm a post office employee—not a detective. All I know is, he's Chinese! Say, miss, you look puzzled. What is this, a Chinese puzzle?" he asked, laughingly.

"Yes, it is," Nancy answered, smiling. "Is the man coming back?"

"How would I know?" the clerk grumbled. Then seeing Nancy was about to leave, he called after her:

"Wait a minute, miss. I just remembered something! That Chinese said he was going to hunt up the other Miles Monroe and get his package!"

CHAPTER XX

The Clue of the Leaning Chimney

"THANKS a lot!" Nancy cried to the postal clerk.

She dashed off to a telephone booth in a near-by store. Within a few seconds she had the professor on the wire. Learning that no Chinese had been there, Nancy told him he might have a visitor and to be on guard. She suggested that he call the police at once if the man should show up for his package.

"I'm pretty sure he's wanted by the police for questioning," Nancy told the geologist.

"Goodness, you're certainly a busy young lady," Miles Monroe gasped, and thanked her for warning him.

Feeling confident that the Oriental was probably the same one who had collected the money orders in Masonville under Mr. Soong's name, she put a call through to her friend Captain McGinnis.

"If he is, he didn't wear a disguise this time,"

Nancy told herself as she waited for an answer. "And I'm sure he's Manning-Carr's brother."

"Hello. Captain McGinnis? Nancy Drew."

Quickly the young detective voiced her suspicions. The officer thought her clue a very important one. "I'll put a man on duty at the post office right away," he told her.

After glancing at her watch, Nancy quickly hurried to her car. She was due at Connie Milton's in five minutes to mind Baby Sue. She hoped Mr. Soong had telephoned the Drew home by now and that Hannah Gruen had told him where he could reach her.

With this latest development of the paints added to the mystery, she could hardly wait to see Mr. Soong. There were *so* many things to tell him!

Connie was somewhat worried about Sue when Nancy arrived at the modest but neat little house. Seeing her mother dressed to go out without showing any signs of taking her along, Sue let out a howl. Nancy calmed Connie's fears laughingly.

"Go on to the party and have a good time!" she said, ushering her toward the door. "I've handled babies before. Now then, young lady," she said, taking the baby in her arms, "you and I will have some fun!"

The baby stared at Nancy with an expression of wondering surprise, then her blue eyes crinkled and her mouth curved into a wide grin.

She played with her a few minutes, then placed the cooing infant in the carriage on the porch. Watching until she saw the baby's eyes slowly close, she tiptoed quietly into the house.

Taking a book from the bookcase, Nancy tried to pass the time in reading. But her mind was too full of the new angle to the mystery for her to absorb the words on the pages. Finally she tossed the book aside and concentrated on her sketch of the iron ornament on the leaning chimney.

"I'm sure the answer to the whole puzzle is in this," she concluded.

When four o'clock came, and she had not heard from Mr. Soong, Nancy was unable to check her mounting curiosity. She went to the telephone and dialed his number. To her delight, the call was answered immediately by the Chinese importer himself.

"I left a message for you to phone me!" Nancy told him, somewhat hurt, when she learned he had been home since eleven o'clock.

"Message?" his soft voice repeated with surprise. "I'm afraid I don't understand."

It was Nancy's turn to feel perplexed.

"Didn't Ching give you my note?" she asked after a moment.

"Ching is not here," Mr. Soong replied. "He must have put the message in his pocket. I will ask him about it when he returns."

Nancy said that she had something important to show Mr. Soong, and he promised to hurry over at once. When he arrived, Nancy told him first of her recent experience inside the enclosure, then showed him her sketch of the iron ornament. Mr. Soong's eyebrows lifted in surprise.

"It is a Chinese symbol," he informed the girl, confirming Nancy's deduction. "But what reason there could be for displaying it on the chimney I do not know."

"Is there any special significance to the symbol?" Nancy asked quickly.

"Very special," Mr. Soong assured her. "It means 'help'!"

" 'Help?' " Nancy repeated.

"Yes." Mr. Soong took a pen from his pocket and printed a word on the back of an envelope. "If it could be written in English, the word would be spelled like this."

Nancy looked at the word. "Phang," she said haltingly.

"No, no," Mr. Soong corrected her. "That is just the way the word is spelled. It is pronounced *bong*."

Nancy stared at him in sudden excitement.

"Bong?" she said at last. "You mean the word is a cry for help?"

"Yes. But I do not understand its use on the leaning chimney."

"I heard such a sound come from near the enclosure!" Nancy announced triumphantly. "A scream that sounded exactly like *bong!*"

Mr. Soong was so mystified by her words, Nancy hastily apprised him of everything she now suspected about the enclosure.

First, that the place was not merely a religious retreat. With or without the knowledge of the Lavender Sisters, the valuable clay was being dug on the property.

"I heard a motor working last night," she said. "They probably dig only at night when outsiders aren't likely to be around."

Second, Nancy went over the double puzzle of the stolen and faked potteries. The rare old pieces, including Mr. Soong's prized Ming vase which had been stolen by a thief known as John Manning. The clever imitations of valuable old potteries, which had been sold by a man named Carr. And the supposition that Manning and Carr were the same person, and used other aliases, perhaps Monroe among them.

Third, Nancy told the importer of finding her missing car in the clearing near the enclosure. Since the car had been stolen by the person who had dropped the jade elephant on the bank of the stream, it looked as if he was associated with the pottery thieves.

Mr. Soong listened intently. "My dear," he

said, "your powers of deduction contain the wisdom of a Chinese philosopher."

Nancy blushed a little. "I'm only putting two and two together," she replied modestly.

Then, last of all, Nancy brought up the subject of Eng Moy and his daughter Eng Lei. Both had vanished mysteriously in the company of a man known as David Carr. Eng Moy's signature had appeared on at least two of the potteries sold by Carr, one of which was doubtless stolen and the other a clever imitation.

"I believe," said Nancy, "that your friends are mixed up with this Carr in the fake pottery making. No doubt they are not willing partners, but they may be the criminal's prisoners in that enclosure!"

Mr. Soong gave a start, then sat for a moment without speaking.

"Thank you for not saying my friends may be part of something dishonest," he said with simple dignity. "I know how damaging the facts must appear. But when the truth is out, I believe in my heart that Eng Moy and Lei will be found to be innocent of any wrongdoing."

Nancy leaned forward. "To save them from further harm, I believe we should notify the police at once," she said.

"Oh, no!" the Chinese cried out. "Not that, please!"

"No?" queried Nancy. "If that place in the woods contains criminals, it's our duty to notify the authorities."

The Chinese wrung his hands. "For the sake of my good friends," he pleaded, "don't tell the police now. Perhaps later. Miss Drew, I implore you to give the Engs a chance to clear their names before they are arrested."

Then he hung his head. "If there were only some way—" He looked at Nancy. "Would you show me the path to the leaning chimney?" he asked pathetically. "I must find out the truth about my friends! Those wretches may kill Moy and Lei so they cannot talk. Please, Miss Drew."

Nancy was touched by the man's sincerity. "You're a real friend," she said. "I'll help you."

"You'll show me the way to the enclosure?"

"Yes," Nancy promised.

"When?"

"Right now. Here comes Connie Milton."

CHAPTER XXI

The Riddle Unravels

It was late in the afternoon when Nancy and Mr. Soong started for the four-walled board enclosure.

When Nancy told Connie Milton where they were going, the young woman strongly objected. But upon being told the trip was only an investigation prior to perhaps calling the police, she felt better.

"Dick has something down cellar you might use to get over the wall," Connie told Nancy. "It's a rope ladder with metal grappling hooks at one end."

Nancy was delighted to have it, since she was not certain the ladder Bess and George had hidden in the woods was still there. In any case it was too heavy for her and Mr. Soong to lift over the board fence and use as a means of escape from the enclosure.

Nancy thanked Connie, put the rope ladder into

her car and set off with Mr. Soong toward the woods. When they arrived at the part of the grounds where the leaning chimney was, Nancy decided to show him the ornament. Walking to the little knoll from which it could be seen, she started to point, then suddenly exclaimed:

"It's gone!"

"What's gone?"

"The Phang ornament!"

Nancy suddenly wondered if she were to blame. It was possible that the person who had put up the symbol had not wanted the Lavender Sisters to know about it. And Nancy had told one of the women!

Quickly she attached the hooks of the rope ladder to the fence, breaking the rusted barbed wire, climbed up, and looked over. With no one in sight in the weed-filled garden, it seemed safe for her and Mr. Soong to drop down inside.

Nancy was worried that he would not be able to do this, but the old gentleman was more agile than she had supposed and dropped lightly to the ground behind her. She hid the ladder beneath a bush and said, pointing:

"We're in luck!"

The wooden door in the stone wall which ran from the old brick building to the fence stood open. Cautiously Nancy and Mr. Soong went through it. Then, keeping in the shelter of the many trees, she led the way to the area where she had seen the lights and heard the engine on her last visit.

They encountered no one but heard muffled thuds. Presently they reached the spot. The sight ahead of them made Nancy's heart beat faster. Her search was rewarded!

There was a shallow pit of sand-colored earth and flintlike layers of rock. Two Chinese, wearing mud-spattered overalls, stood ankle-deep in the pit, breaking up the rock with sledge hammers. Another man scooped up the yellowish soil with a shovel, while a fourth workman carried away the soil and broken pieces of shale in a wheelbarrow.

To Nancy the rocks had the hard, gray look of granite, and she turned to Mr. Soong to confirm the thought that followed her observation.

"There's kaolin in it?" she whispered, with a nod toward the pit.

Mr. Soong bobbed his head excitedly. "A high percentage. Excellent for making porcelain."

But Nancy did not allow her elation to overshadow the main reason for her coming to the secret spot. She must still hunt for the Engs.

"Come on!" she whispered to her companion.

As Mr. Soong started to follow her, he stepped on a dry branch which cracked with a sound like a pistol shot. Instantly the diggers looked up.

Nancy, dismayed, pulled Mr. Soong to the ground behind a bush and looked between its branches to watch what the workmen would do. One stared straight at the shrub that concealed them!

He turned to a second digger and said something Nancy could not hear. The second workman shrugged and to Nancy's relief returned to his shovel. After a moment of puzzled deliberation, the other followed suit.

Nancy felt Mr. Soong relax beside her and he gave her an apologetic smile.

"Forgive me for being so clumsy," he said. "I will not give away our presence again."

Keeping well hidden, Nancy led the Chinese from one part of the grounds to another, hoping, with each step they took, that the huge mastiff would not appear.

They passed a small bungalow and several pitched tents but saw no one. Finally Nancy concluded that probably the Lavender Sisters and any others in the enclosure besides the diggers must be inside the mysterious brick building.

"We'll go back there," she told Mr. Soong.

The building was some distance from where they now were, and Nancy was fearful Mr. Soong could not stand so much walking. But he surprised her by stepping along without showing any

signs of weariness. He must have guessed her
thoughts, for he said:

"In China no one grows weary in body if he is
helping a friend."

Nancy liked this bit of philosophy, and walked
faster. Upon reaching the brick building with the
leaning chimney, Mr. Soong stared at it hopefully.

The door was closed, and the small dust-covered
windows much too high for anyone to look inside.
There were no sounds coming from within.

"We'll go closer," Nancy suggested.

As she stepped forward, the door of the brick
building, less than forty feet away, suddenly swung
back and a slender, pretty Chinese girl about
Nancy's age appeared on the steps.

The girl's hair was dark and radiant, parted
simply in the center of her well-shaped head. It
was gathered into two round, neat buns at the nape
of her neck. She wore a clay-spattered canvas
apron over a plain gray cotton dress.

The young Chinese girl stood for a moment,
looking toward the direction of the pit, then suddenly she burst into tears.

"That may be Eng Lei!" Nancy thought.

A man came through the doorway and put his
arm around the girl's shoulder soothingly. He
spoke to her softly in Chinese.

Mr. Soong's fingers suddenly closed tightly over Nancy's wrist and she saw as she turned that his eyes were fixed excitedly on the man.

"It is my friend!" he whispered. "It is Eng Moy!"

He started to dash forward, but Nancy held him back.

"Before we show ourselves, we must find out what his position is here and be sure that he won't betray us," she whispered warningly.

Mr. Soong's face fell, then he smiled.

"My heart is so full of the desire to greet my old friend," he said apologetically, "I am afraid my head is forgetful. I will try to be more careful."

Nancy pressed his arm reassuringly as she studied the middle-aged Eng Moy. Coarse blue-denim work clothes, splashed with white clay, hung loosely on his thin, frail body. His face, as he spoke comfortingly to the girl, showed a quiet resignation that told of long suffering.

"The girl must be Eng Lei," Nancy murmured to Mr. Soong, her heart going out to the old gentleman as his eyes reflected the tension under which he was laboring.

He nodded eagerly. "I think you are right. But so many years have passed since I last saw Lei —she was only a child in pigtails when I left China many years ago—I cannot be sure."

"What are they saying?" Nancy whispered as

Eng Moy again spoke softly to the girl in Chinese.

Mr. Soong shook his head helplessly.

"I cannot hear," he confessed.

A moment later the Engs turned back into the building. Nancy and Mr. Soong stole swiftly and cautiously through the entrance after them.

CHAPTER XXII

Reunion

THE room in which Nancy and Mr. Soong found themselves was small and dimly lighted. It contained nothing but a few crates stacked near a doorway which led to a large, better lighted room. In it a wide workbench was arranged along one wall. On this lay tubes of paint and bowls of turpentine containing brushes.

Lined along the rear of the workbench were two neat rows of porcelain bowls, jugs, jars and vases; all glazed and beautifully decorated with Oriental designs. Above them on the wall were cabinets, their doors closed.

Eng Moy and his daughter Lei took their places at the workbench, their backs to the door. They picked up the delicate designing brushes and began working on two gracefully shaped potteries of white porcelain. Lei was concentrating on a half-painted china teapot. Her father—Nancy's breath quickened and she bent closer to Mr. Soong's ear.

"Look at the vase Eng Moy just took from the cabinet!" she directed. "Doesn't it look familiar?"

Mr. Soong's eyes fixed on the vase.

"Why, it's mine!" he whispered excitedly. "It's the vase stolen from young Milton's shop!"

"Exactly," confirmed Nancy. "And if you look closely you'll see why Manning-Carr wanted it. Eng Moy is copying it—and probably made the copy which Manning-Carr sold in New York."

At that moment the Lavender Sister, who had ordered Nancy away from the enclosure some days before, entered the room through a far doorway. She gave the Engs a hostile glance, then bent to examine their work. Suddenly she pointed to a small jar and uttered a stream of Chinese in a harsh, shrill voice.

Stepping swiftly toward Lei, before the father could intervene, she slapped the cowering girl's face. Then she turned abruptly and departed through the same doorway from which she had appeared.

Nancy caught a fleeting glimpse of the interior beyond. It seemed to contain pottery-making equipment.

As the door closed, Nancy heard the sound of weeping. It came from Lei, whose pretty face was contorted with bitterness and shame. Once more Eng Moy attempted to comfort his daughter, but she resisted his soothing words.

Mr. Soong, listening to the exchange of Chinese, translated it to Nancy exactly as it had been spoken.

"Father, I cannot stand this hateful life any longer!" Lei sobbed. "I wish I had never been born!"

"You must not talk that way, my child," Eng Moy remonstrated gently. "You are too young and beautiful to give up hope."

"Hope!" the girl replied bitterly. "Day after day, year after year I have lived because of that word! Hoping for rescue! Hoping for the capture and punishment of the men who keep us here! Hoping to see China and home again! I tell you, Father, it is no use! Hope for us is an empty word. I never want to hear it again!"

His face eloquent with distress, Eng Moy turned away.

"But what can we do?" he muttered helplessly.

"We have only one choice left, Father," Lei told him. "We must end it all, rather than spend our lives in misery. It is our only means of escape."

"No! Never that!" Mr. Soong cried out in Chinese.

He came from behind the crates and went quickly toward the Engs, followed by Nancy. Surprise flashed across Lei's face, then she backed away in sudden fear.

Mr. Soong went directly to Eng Moy and embraced him.

"My friend! My old friend!" he murmured huskily.

Eng Moy drew back and stared at the old gentleman. Then slowly a look of recognition dawned on his face.

"Soong!" he whispered disbelievingly.

His eyes blinked in bewilderment, as if unable to credit what they saw. Then he stepped forward with a happy cry and returned Mr. Soong's embrace.

Introductions quickly followed. Then, smiling proudly at Nancy, Mr. Soong spoke rapidly to the Engs. When he had finished, they turned to the girl, their faces reflecting gratitude and hope.

Eng Moy took Nancy's hands in his and addressed her haltingly in Chinese, while Lei stood by and smiled in agreement with her father's soft-spoken words.

Despite the barrier of languages that stood between them—for the Engs could neither speak nor understand English—Nancy and the Chinese father and daughter became friends at once.

"What are they trying to tell me?" Nancy asked Mr. Soong.

"They wish to thank you for bringing me here," the old gentleman replied.

"There'll be time enough for that when we're all safely out of the enclosure," Nancy said. "We must hurry away before we're caught!"

Ever mindful that their presence might be detected at any moment, she had Mr. Soong explain her plan of escape to the Engs—a plan whereby all four of them would climb over the fence at the point where she and her companion had hidden the ladder. The Engs looked at each other, as if escape were beyond their wildest dreams, then nodded eagerly to show Nancy they understood.

Leading the way to the door, Nancy pulled it open a crack and cautiously peered outside. A second later she caught her breath.

Coming toward the old brick building was a man with black hair and dark skin. But the most striking thing about him was his eyes. They seemed to stare from his head like two small, glittering black marbles. Nancy, though she had never met him, was sure she knew his identity. However, she asked:

"Who is he?"

Mr. Soong, getting the answer from the Engs, confirmed her suspicion. The man was David Carr! Nancy closed the door quickly.

"Tell the Engs they must hide us!" Nancy said to Mr. Soong.

Eng Moy and Lei looked stunned at the turn of events. They stood still.

"Let's take a chance on that room beyond," Nancy suggested quickly.

Eng Moy said he would run ahead and see if

any men or women were in it. He reported two women were at work there.

Nancy glanced through the window. Carr had stopped to inspect something on the ground. A moment's breather!

"Ask the Engs if they can let us have some old work clothes, Mr. Soong," she instructed. "We'll take a chance getting past those women."

The Chinese quickly translated. Hurrying to a row of hooks jutting from the wall, Lei brought back a clay-spattered apron for Nancy and a similarly messy pair of overalls for Mr. Soong.

"Hurry!" Nancy said to him. "Carr may come in here any minute!"

They swiftly slipped the garments over their own clothing and Nancy wound a scarf around her yellow-blonde hair. Then she quickly studied the results.

"I think we'll pass," she told Mr. Soong, "as long as we stay in the shadows where we won't be clearly seen."

She opened the door to the workshop. Then, taking a deep breath, she stepped into the shop and started along the shadowy wall toward the opposite end of the room where there was still another door.

Nancy walked as casually as she could, her face slightly averted from the women, who stood at tables pounding clay. After a moment Nancy noted gratefully that Lei had slipped up beside her to help screen her from suspicious stares. Behind her were Eng Moy and Mr. Soong.

Two or three times the women workers looked up at them curiously but showed no signs of suspecting anything amiss. At last the little group arrived at the end of the shop.

Going through a doorway into a short corridor, Nancy saw a large iron door. The Engs whispered something and Mr. Soong translated for Nancy.

"Behind the door is a brick vault containing genuine old Chinese porcelains, all of them stolen," he explained. "Only Carr and his brother possess keys to the vault."

Nancy felt a twinge of excitement. The mystery was unraveling fast now! And this was the first real evidence she had that the swindler's brother was working with him!

The group had stopped, safe for the moment. Then terror struck their hearts. Outside the wall where the four were huddled the horrible mastiff began to bay.

Had an alarm been given?

CHAPTER XXIII

Meeting the Enemy

NANCY had assumed there was another door in the building, and she was right. But escape through it now was impossible.

Mr. Soong explained the danger to the Engs. The two Chinese, who had begun to believe that their imprisonment might indeed be at an end, were plunged into gloom once more.

"Our only chance is to hide until the dog is taken away," Nancy said to Mr. Soong. "Ask your friends if there's a place where we can wait without too much risk of being detected."

The elderly man did this, and Eng Moy led them to a small room at the extreme rear corner of the building. He pointed to a battered old brick wall. Studying it in the faint light, Nancy could not imagine what possible hiding place the wall could provide.

Walking to the end of it, Eng Moy pulled open

a rusted iron door in the wall. As it creaked back on rusty hinges, he stepped into a dank, dark cavern and lighted a candle. Then, turning, he motioned to the others to follow.

Nancy exclaimed in surprise. They were standing in a large, dome-shaped area about eight feet high at the center. The circular brick wall was dilapidated and battered, and the rough stone flooring cracked. Nancy noticed that the roof of the oven funneled at the center into the leaning chimney.

"This must have been the smelter of the old Civil War iron mine!" she told Mr. Soong excitedly.

The old gentleman spoke a few words to Eng Moy.

"You are right, my dear," he reported. "Eng Moy says the old mine is on these grounds, and this building was in use at that time. When Eng Moy came to the enclosure, this old smelter was used as a kiln to fire pottery. But it seemed as if the chimney would topple over at any time, so a modern kiln was constructed across the garden."

Lei went off to stand watch at the far door, to give notice the instant anyone might come along the corridor. Nancy, Eng Moy and Mr. Soong sat down on the floor inside the old smelter to await a favorable time to escape. As they marked time, the thin, frail pottery maker haltingly told his

Chinese friend all that had happened to him and his daughter since they had arrived in San Francisco five years before.

So slowly did he speak, and so often did he stop to master his emotions, Mr. Soong had no difficulty in retelling the story to Nancy almost as soon as it was told to him.

The man known to him as David Carr, Eng Moy said, had been a business acquaintance in China. He had tricked the Engs into coming to America by making the father honeyed promises of an important position in one of the country's modern pottery plants. As the final stop in their tour of American factories, Carr had lured them to the enclosure in the woods, and there made them prisoners.

The Engs had lived in captivity ever since, four and a half long, miserable years. During that time they had been forced to design fake Chinese potteries, using as their models genuine, rare old Oriental porcelains that Carr had stolen.

"But surely the Engs tried to escape?" Nancy exclaimed.

Mr. Soong translated her remark, then turned back to the girl.

"Yes, many times," he told Nancy. "Twice they even reached the woods outside the board fence before their absence was discovered. But the dog soon found them, and their poor bodies

still bear the marks of the whip Carr used to pun-
ish them."

Nancy's ire was aroused anew. Poor Lei and her
father had been the victims of extreme cruelty.

"Then it was Lei I heard scream for help?"
Nancy asked. "The cry that sounded like *bong?*"

"Yes," Mr. Soong answered. "The two Phang
characters you saw attached to the chimney also
were appeals for help. Eng put them there, hoping to attract someone's attention. He shaped the
characters out of old scraps of iron he found. The
ornament you saw first had been attached to the
chimney for so long it had rusted, and most of its
crosspieces had fallen off."

"That, of course, is why Eng took it down,"
Nancy observed. "But who removed the new
ornament?"

"My friend was compelled to remove it the day
he put it up," Mr. Soong said. "One of the Lavender Sisters saw it and punished him."

Nancy's conscience pricked her. *She* had told
the woman about it, and no doubt caused his punishment! Quickly Nancy had Mr. Soong explain
this and offered her regrets.

"Eng Moy says he is so glad you saw it, the of-
fense does not matter," Mr. Soong translated.
"The clue of the leaning chimney is the means of
your saving the lives of himself and Lei."

"Saving their lives?"

"Carr told them," Mr. Soong went on, "that if anyone ever found out the secret of this place he would kill everyone in it, so they could not talk, and then he himself would run away."

"He's one of the cruelest crooks I've ever known," Nancy said, and added to herself, "If he finds us here, I'm afraid . . ."

Her thoughts were interrupted as Mr. Soong continued to translate. She was told that Eng Moy's signature, cunningly worked into the designs of various pieces of pottery, had also been intended by him as an appeal for aid.

Carr had made sure his prisoners were given no opportunity to learn English, so Eng Moy had used the only effective means at his disposal. Knowing that government authorities would be trying to locate him for illegally remaining in America, Eng Moy hoped one of the signatures would come to the attention of Federal officers and lead them to the enclosure.

"My friend would never deface a rare, old porcelain," Mr. Soong explained. "His signature can be removed easily with no harm to the piece."

"The other people," Nancy said suddenly, "the men and women we saw working in the pit and in the shop. Are they prisoners, too?"

Mr. Soong turned inquiringly to Eng Moy, then sat silently for a moment after his friend had supplied the explanation.

"What did he say?" Nancy queried with Yankee impatience.

The gentle Chinese gave her a troubled look.

"The men are foreigners," he told her. "The women are their wives. Carr and his brother smuggled them into the United States by plane."

Another count against this fiendish crook!

"Poor, foolish, misguided people!" Mr. Soong went on with a shake of his head. "Carr promised them wonderful things, then he made them prisoners. Finally he threatened if they did not dig the clay and operate the machines, he would expose them to the police and have them put in jail for life!"

At that moment they heard the iron door squeak open. Lei slipped into the candlelit smelter. She spoke breathlessly to her father and from the sudden fear that flitted across his face Nancy knew something had gone wrong.

"The Engs' absence has been discovered!" Mr. Soong told her with alarm. "Lei overheard one of the Lavender Sisters report it to Carr, who's her husband."

"Quick!" Nancy said. "Tell the Engs to show themselves outside! They can join us here later and we'll escape then."

The Chinese spoke rapidly to his friends, and they crept into the corridor. But hardly had the Engs gone when they reappeared.

"Why have they come back?" Nancy asked, puzzled.

"They cannot leave now without betraying our hiding place!" Mr. Soong explained. "Carr and the woman are out in the corridor!"

Motioning to the others to wait, Nancy stole from the old smelter into the shadowy room outside and listened. Soon she heard voices.

"You fool!" cried a man's voice. "If you'd paid more attention to the Engs, they couldn't have disappeared!"

"They can't have gone far!" the Lavender Sister replied.

"The mastiff!" Carr cried out sharply. "We must pick up their trail at once!"

Nancy's heart sank. If the mastiff traced the Engs' scent to the iron smelter, she and Mr. Soong would be discovered too and all would be lost.

Suddenly Carr ordered, "Wait! Whose handkerchief is this?"

"Eng Lei's," his wife declared.

"Get the dog," Carr said shortly. "She and that father of hers are probably in the smelter room. My mastiff will attend to them!"

Nancy turned and ran softly back to the smelter. Slipping through the partially open door, she closed it as quietly as possible behind her.

"They're coming!" she whispered.

Eng Moy blew out the candle, and the four

waited with mounting suspense in the dark. Then, after an interval that seemed to be years, a voice spoke sharply in Chinese outside the iron door.

"It is Carr!" Mr. Soong whispered fearfully to Nancy. "He demands that the Engs come out! What shall we do?" he asked in panic.

Before she could reply that it would be best for them to slip out without betraying her and Soong's presence, the door was pulled open.

Carr stepped into the doorway and flashed a light about. An expression of utmost surprise flitted over his swarthy face as he saw Nancy and Mr. Soong. But he recovered himself in a moment, and his thin lips spread in a slow, mocking smile.

"So! I have caught you at last!" he said sarcastically, his glittering black eyes moving from the girl to her Chinese companion and then back again.

The Lavender Sister, who arrived with the mastiff, gave a dry, harsh chuckle when she saw Nancy.

"You did not believe me when I warned you," she said. "Now the evil spirits will attend to you as I said."

"Be quiet!" her husband ordered her. "Take the Engs away and make sure they do not try to escape again."

The woman beckoned sharply to the thin, frail pottery maker and his pretty daughter. With a despairing glance at Nancy and Mr. Soong, they followed Carr's wife through the doorway.

Nancy watched them go with a heavy heart. How happy they had been when freedom seemed so near, she reflected. And how utterly defeated they now appeared.

Carr studied Nancy and her companion silently, then spoke again.

"I'm sure you want to know what I intend to do with you, so I won't keep you in suspense," he said. His eyes flickered over the old iron mine oven. "The simplest thing would be to lock you in this old smelter and let you starve . . ."

"You wouldn't dare!" Nancy burst out.

"There isn't anything I wouldn't dare do to eliminate you, Miss Drew!" he said in a cold, sharp, metallic voice. "Furthermore, I intend to do it before any of your friends can get here to help you!"

CHAPTER XXIV

Escape

AT DAVID CARR's harsh words, Mr. Soong moaned.

"Nobody," shouted Carr angrily, "is going to interfere with me and get away with it! You, Nancy Drew, have interfered with my plans since the first time you saw me on Three Bridges Road."

"And I'll keep on interfering—until you and your brother are locked behind bars!" Nancy retorted.

Carr's face tightened. "Ah! So you know about my brother?"

"I do!" Nancy declared. "And I know all about his activities, too!" She took a shot at random, hoping it would induce the swindler to expose his brother's identity.

Instead, Carr gave her a thin-lipped smile and said:

"You are very clever. Since you probably know it, I'll admit those were my brother's footprints

you found after he stole the vase from the Townsends and the jade elephant from your home."

Nancy nodded. "Why did he bother to steal
the vase when he knew it was a fake?"

The swindler's swarthy face twitched in anger.
"My wife is to blame for that!" he replied harshly.
"Because of her stupidity, Eng Moy was able to
paint his name on several porcelains I sold. My
brother and I stole back as many as we could. We
were afraid the signature would be recognized and
traced by Federal dicks."

"Of course!" Nancy explained. "That's why
you stole the Townsend vase. You managed to remove Eng's name and sold the vase again. But
who posed as Mr. Soong to collect the money
orders in Masonville?" she asked quickly, hoping
to catch Carr off guard. "Your brother?"

The crook was much too cagey, however, to refer
to his confederate by name. He addressed his reply tauntingly to the old Chinese gentleman, who
stood listening close by.

"That was clever, eh, Soong? It's just too bad
for Miss Drew his scheme didn't completely suc-
ceed. If she'd believed you guilty of selling fake
potteries, she might have stopped meddling in my
affairs and wouldn't be here now to face the con-
sequences!"

"I'm glad I was able to help Mr. Soong," Nancy
declared hotly.

Carr gave a mirthless, sardonic laugh.

"Later," he told the girl, "you will sing a different tune!" He turned to go. "I advise you not to try to escape," he warned. "The mastiff has a nasty temper and very sharp fangs! I'll be back in a few minutes and then we'll see how brave you are!"

He swung the iron door shut. Nancy found the candle and lighted it. She turned to Mr. Soong who had sat down on the floor, too weak to stand any longer.

"It's my fault you're in this dangerous situation," he told her in self-reproach. "I shouldn't have asked you to come with me."

Nancy smiled wanly. "Please do not feel bad. It was my own wish to untangle this mystery that brought us here."

Mr. Soong shook his head gently. "My dear," he said, "the Engs are my friends and I could never have forgiven myself if I had not done everything in my power to help them. But for you to risk—" He broke off, his voice failing.

"Please do not worry about me," Nancy begged. She crossed to the door to listen, hoping the dog might be gone. But the mastiff outside, sensing her presence near the iron barrier, uttered a low, menacing growl.

Nancy took the candle and started to examine the battered bricks walls. There *had* to be some way of escape!

Suddenly the iron door creaked slowly open. They looked swiftly at the entrance, expecting to see Carr, but gasped in openmouthed surprise at the newcomer.

Standing in the doorway was Mr. Soong's short, inscrutable-looking servant, Ching! He regarded them impassively, then gave them a toothy smile.

"Ching!" Mr. Soong arose and advanced toward him eagerly. "Ching, you've come to save us!"

He spoke excitedly to the servant in Chinese. But Ching suddenly gave a boisterous laugh and pushed the old gentleman away so roughly he fell to the floor.

"Fool!" he cried in unexpected English. "Do you think I came here to help you? You and your snooping, spying friend? Do you believe I am nothing more than a servant? Are you so stupid you cannot guess who I really am?"

"Carr's brother!" The words slipped from Nancy's lips almost before she realized what she was saying.

Ching made her a mock bow. "Exactly!" he said.

Nancy, who had been helping Mr. Soong to regain his feet, stared at the sneering, triumphant ex-servant.

"Now I understand several things," she said half-aloud. "You were the one who posed as Mr. Soong and cashed the money orders!"

"Yes, Miss Drew," Ching replied mockingly. "But my impersonation need not concern you any longer. You made a fatal mistake in coming here. Now you must pay for your stupidity." He chuckled contemptuously. "There is an old American saying, 'Curiosity killed the cat.' You see the parallel, Miss Drew, I'm sure. Like the cat, you have become far too nosy for your own good."

"There's no use threatening us. You know my father will come and bring the police!" Nancy burst out.

"Wouldn't you like us to believe that, Miss Drew?" Ching taunted. "But unfortunately for you, I know that your father is in Washington. You see, I called his office, intending to tell him that you would be—er—slightly late for dinner."

Nancy realized how serious her plight was, but there was a ray of hope. When she did not return to dinner, Mrs. Gruen certainly would telephone the Miltons, and when the housekeeper learned that Nancy and Mr. Soong had gone to the enclosure, she would call the police.

Sparring for time, she continued to ask questions which Ching freely answered.

He said it had been prearranged between David and himself that he would get a job at Mr. Soong's. In this way he could watch the man's mail and waylay any messages about the Engs. At all times he kept track of his employer's movements.

"But once you slipped," Nancy spoke up. "A letter about the Engs did reach Mr. Soong."

"Unfortunately, yes. Then you came into the case, Miss Drew. But you shall never bother my brother or me again. In a short time he and I will be gone from here. But first, we will destroy all evidence against us. That includes people who would talk about our work."

Mr. Soong spoke in Chinese to his former servant. His pleas to let Nancy go, if no one else, fell on deaf ears.

"As soon as my brother and I have removed our valuable property," Ching said defiantly, "we will come back and dynamite the leaning chimney. When it collapses, it will crush the roof of the smelter." He paused significantly. "Your fate will not be pleasant. But let us hope the end will be swift!"

For several seconds after Ching had departed, Nancy and Mr. Soong were too dazed by the meaning of his words even to talk. It occurred to Nancy that Mrs. Gruen would not be concerned about her absence until the dinner hour. The housekeeper would act promptly then, but it might be too late. Desperately, Nancy began to try to figure some way out of their dreadful plight.

"There isn't a chance of escaping through the door with the mastiff on guard," she pointed out to herself.

Mr. Soong sat in silence. Every few seconds he

would sigh. Nancy was afraid he might collapse any minute.

Holding the candle above her head, Nancy stared at the domelike roof of the old smelter. The hole where it funneled into the leaning chimney was about two feet in diameter. Through the opening she could just see a patch of sunlit sky. A subconscious thought clicked into place and she turned excitedly to Mr. Soong.

"Didn't Eng Moy get up the inside of the chimney to attach the iron symbol?" she asked.

The elderly gentleman, his mind still full of their impending fate, looked at her in bewilderment, but at last he replied:

"Yes. He said he used a ladder and went up from here."

There was no ladder in the smelter. Nancy peered again up the chimney. Ladder or no ladder, she promptly decided to try the climb.

"Please help me get up," she said, telling the aged Chinese her plan.

Mr. Soong's eyes widened. "You don't intend to climb the chimney?" he asked in alarm.

"I must!" Nancy told him. "It's our only chance of escape."

"But you might slip and fall! You might be seriously hurt; even worse!"

"Nothing would be worse than the fate that awaits us here," Nancy pointed out. "But if I can make the climb, I may be able to bring help to you and your friends before it's too late."

Recognizing that there was no choice, the Chinese leaned down and, exerting his last ounce of strength, permitted the girl to stand on his back so she could reach into the opening. As Nancy pulled herself up inside, Mr. Soong looked at her anxiously.

"Be careful," he begged. "If anything should happen to you—"

"I'll try to take care that nothing does," Nancy reassured him. "And don't give up hope. If everything goes well, I'll be back with the police."

"Good fortune go with you!" said Mr. Soong, sinking to the floor.

Nancy started her climb. Bracing her back against one side of the chimney and her legs against the other, she started to inch up the stack like an inchworm.

Her climb was made easier by the angle at which the chimney slanted. But the cement between the bricks was chipped and broken. With every movement she made, Nancy was in danger of dislodging a loose brick and plunging down the dank shaft to the floor of the smelter!

With utmost care, she crept upward. Finally, when it seemed as if her tense, tired muscles would carry her no farther, she reached the top. Then she climbed carefully down the outside of the leaning chimney to the sloping roof of the old brick building.

She was about to make the eight-foot drop from the edge of the roof to the garden when she heard a sneeze.

"Someone's coming!" she thought with alarm.

Swiftly Nancy flattened herself against the sloping roof, and a moment later saw Carr's wife, now in street clothes, open the door in the stone wall and walk in her direction.

As long as the woman did not look up, Nancy was safe from view. But the angle at which the roof sloped made her position precarious. As Carr's wife approached, Nancy's grip suddenly weakened and she started to slide down.

"I can't fail now!" she told herself desperately. "I just can't!"

CHAPTER XXV

A Fitting Reward

FRANTICALLY, she pressed her hands harder against the roof, and just when it seemed she must tumble to the ground, her momentum stopped.

Carr's wife paused to listen, but evidently did not detect the sound as coming from the roof, because she did not look up. Finally the woman returned to the door in the stone wall and went through.

Nancy breathed with relief. Landing lightly on the spongy turf below the roof, she ran to where she had hidden the rope ladder. It was still there. Nancy placed it against the wooden fence and climbed over quickly.

She tossed the ladder behind a tree and ran headlong, staying away from the end of the enclosure where the gate was. Taking a circuitous route to avoid detection, she finally came to the parked car. She jumped in and drove as swiftly as possible along the gravel lane; then raced toward Three Bridges Road.

As Nancy was about to turn into the road, she uttered an exclamation of relief. Crossing the intersection not twenty feet in front of her was the familiar car of a state trooper!

Nancy blew a long blast on her horn and the police car stopped. She slipped out of the convertible and ran toward the trooper.

"Thank goodness you're here!" she told him. "I need help—right away!"

"What's wrong, miss?"

Nancy apprised him of the situation at the enclosure.

"Looks like we'll need plenty of help," the trooper said grimly.

He radioed his district headquarters, and after a short wait they were joined by six state troopers in a patrol car. With Nancy leading the way, they sped toward the enclosure.

The men went over the fence at various locations to make their roundup of the enclosure's inhabitants complete. Nancy and two of the officers went at once to the old brick building to free Mr. Soong.

None of the crooks was in sight, but the two women clay workers, still at their benches, were arrested. Since neither of them could speak English, they could tell the police nothing about Carr and his brother.

"You'll have an ugly dog to tackle in a minute," Nancy warned the troopers as they went on toward the old smelter.

"We'll take care of him."

To Nancy's surprise the mastiff was gone. Nancy was puzzled. What of Mr. Soong? She raced to the door of the smelter and yanked it open. The place was empty.

"He's been taken away!" she cried despairingly.

The troopers looked at her. Had they come too late?

Nancy had a sudden inspiration.

"I believe I know where everybody is," she said.

She led the men to the large corridor vault where Eng Moy had said the valuable potteries were locked up. As Nancy expected, the door would not open, but she could detect a faint whine from within. She told the men she suspected the crooks and their mastiff were inside.

"Come out of there at once!" one of the troopers commanded.

There was utter silençe. Suddenly Nancy realized that if her Chinese friends were inside with the crooks, they might be afraid to answer. So she called loudly:

"It's Nancy Drew! I'm here!"

From inside came a cry of joy from Eng Lei, but

it was stifled at once. The troopers said they would batter down the door if it were not opened immediately!

At last from the interior of the vault, their faces sullen, came Carr, holding the dog by his leash, his wife and Ching. Behind them were Mr. Soong and the Engs, who blinked happily.

The story was soon told. When Carr had discovered Nancy gone, he had rounded up his wife and brother to make a getaway. But Nancy had arrived with the police too soon. By hiding in the vault, Carr had hoped to make the group think he and Ching and the others already had gone.

Before leaving, the Carrs would have disposed of the old Chinese and his friends. The workers outside did not know enough to give very damaging evidence against the brothers.

"You wicked, meddlesome creature!" Carr's wife burst out, pointing a finger at Nancy. "You're to blame for our capture! In another year we would have become rich enough to leave this place forever. But you had to come snooping and spoil it all!"

At that moment another of the troopers approached to report that all the workers in the place had been captured. Nancy quickly introduced Mr. Soong, who was allowed to go. All the others would have to be held for questioning, the officer said, but he was sure the Engs would be allowed to stay at Mr. Soong's home.

"Tell Eng Moy and Eng Lei good-bye for me, Mr. Soong, please," Nancy said with a smile.

"But you will see them again," the old importer promised. "They will not return to China at once."

Next day Mr. Drew, back from Washington, and thankful his daughter was safe, talked over the mystery with Nancy. The Carrs and Ching, they learned from the police, had signed a complete confession.

"One of the things I'm most curious about," Nancy remarked, "is how Carr and Ching obtained possession of the enclosure."

Mr. Drew showed her a copy of the confession. It said the discoverer of the kaolin had been the half-caste brothers' great-grandfather. His son had worked the pit for a while but had moved away. Then his son, the father of David and Ching, had gone to China as a merchant, and the property had been sold for taxes but never used.

Records, testifying to the existence and location of the pit, had lain untouched in an old trunk in Shanghai for many years. Then, five years before, David Carr and his brother had found the records and immediately come to America to look over the pit. Using the name of the geologist, Miles Monroe, to avoid any suspicion, Carr had purchased the tract of land, despite the fact that it did not have a clear title.

"Here's something interesting," Nancy spoke up.

The Carrs had later found out that a man named Petersen had left some papers which might upset their claim to the pit. David had been given a lead to the former owner of Mrs. Wendell's house in Masonville, and this was the telephone conversation Dick Milton had overheard six months ago.

Carr, using the name Manning, had gone to her home, quizzed her about the trunk, taken a room, and stolen the papers he wanted, as Nancy had guessed. He had installed the secret panel leading to the empty attic next door, to keep some of the valuable potteries there, in case the enclosure in the woods was raided.

"You spiked that one early in the game, Nancy." Mr. Drew grinned. "And you thought all along that the religious colony was just a camouflage."

"Well, in a way, the leaning chimney in Masonville was a lucky coincidence." Nancy smiled. "If I hadn't found that, I might not have uncovered the secret of the enclosure."

A week later Mr. Soong held a party in honor of the Engs. He greeted his guests at the door, attired in a colorful embroidered mandarin coat.

Next to greet Nancy and Mr. Drew were the

Engs. After them there was a succession of old friends, including Bess and George, Dick and Connie, and Ned Nickerson, who bemoaned the fact he had not been on hand to take a hand in capturing the crooks.

Nancy noted with satisfaction that displayed on the living room mantel were Mr. Soong's jade elephant and the dragon Ming vase which had been recovered from the swindlers.

After dinner, Mr. Soong made a short, touching speech expressing the debt of gratitude he and the Engs owed Nancy. Then Lei stepped forward, holding in her hands an exquisite vase.

Against a soft green background was pictured a slender, golden-haired girl in a suit of armor, pitting a lance at a scaly green dragon. Behind her stood a Chinese girl and two men in long Oriental robes.

As Lei presented the vase to a surprised Nancy with a warm smile, she spoke in Chinese.

"What is she saying?" Nancy appealed to Mr. Soong.

"Lei is trying to tell you that she and her father made this for you. Like all Chinese work the design tells a story," he explained. "The girl in armor is Nancy Drew. The three Chinese are Lei, Moy and myself whom you are protecting from the evil dragon. The dragon is Ching, Carr and his wife."

"The dragon is all three?" Nancy asked.

"You see," Soong explained, "the dragon has three claws on each foot."

He turned the vase bottom up. Painted on the base were several Chinese characters.

"Why—there's a hallmark!" Nancy cried.

Mr. Soong whispered softly, "It says, 'Made in the hearts of Eng Moy and Eng Lei.'"

Nancy winked back a suspicious wetness from her lashes.

"It's lovely," she whispered. Her glance went to two other symbols painted on the base. "And these?" she asked.

"They are the Chinese characters for the name Lei has given you," Mr. Soong told the girl. "It is pronounced Hsiu Lan. It means 'Graceful Orchid'!"

"Graceful Orchid," Nancy repeated slowly. "What a beautiful name."

"Yes," the old gentleman agreed. "It is one of the most charming names in my country's language, and it could not be bestowed more fittingly."

"Thank you," Nancy said simply. "Thank you very much."

She started to turn away, but there was a burst of applause from the smiling circle of guests.

"Speech!" George prompted, spurring the others to even greater hand clapping.

Nancy looked helplessly at Mr. Soong.

"Please do," he urged, smiling.

"Go ahead, Nancy," Ned spoke up.

"I'll do my best," she promised with a little laugh. "There aren't any words to express the way I feel about this vase. It's already more to me than just a gift, much, much more. It's a token of friendship; a bond between me and three of the nicest people I've ever known. I'll treasure it always."

Applause burst out again as she finished, then the circle broke up and Nancy found herself in one corner of the room with Bess, George and Ned.

"Hypers!" said George. "That was *some* gift. I think I'll start looking for leaning chimneys and people who are crying for help, and see what *I* can dig up."

The others laughed.

"Well, Nancy," said Ned with a teasing grin, "now that you've located the China clay and the missing Engs, what are you going to do next?"

"Next," Nancy replied, "I'm going to tell you a secret. Mr. Soong is lending Dick the money to acquire the China clay, and the Engs are going to stay in America—for a while at least—and work with him making potteries. And now that you know this secret," she added, laughing, "I'm ready and willing to take on any new mystery that comes along."

Although Nancy did not then know it, the mystery was to be the baffling, exciting adventure of "The Secret of the Wooden Lady."

"Meanwhile," Nancy whispered to Bess, "I think I'll join you in the ceramics class. Now that I've learned from Ching and Carr what *not* to do in making potteries, I'd better take a few tips from Dick on what *to* do!"

Victorei Eileen ~~Gilber~~
Gilbert